Theodore Tilton

Thou and I: a Lyric of Human Life

With other Poems

Theodore Tilton

Thou and I: a Lyric of Human Life
With other Poems

ISBN/EAN: 9783744784153

Printed in Europe, USA, Canada, Australia, Japan

Cover: Foto ©Andreas Hilbeck / pixelio.de

More available books at **www.hansebooks.com**

Theodore Tilton

THOU AND I:

A LYRIC OF HUMAN LIFE.

WITH

OTHER POEMS.

BY

THEODORE TILTON.

———

NEW YORK:

R. WORTHINGTON, 750 BROADWAY.

MDCCCLXXX.

This Book

I INSCRIBE TO MY DEAR DAUGHTERS,

FLORENCE AND ALICE,

AS A

TESTIMONY TO THEIR FILIAL DEVOTION,

AND A

TOKEN OF THEIR FATHER'S LOVE.

CONTENTS.

CONTENTS.

SHORTER POEMS—(*Continued.*)

PROEM.

Go, little book, a pilgrim through the land,
And beg a minstrel's welcome here and there ;
But be content, however thou shalt fare,—
In cottage lowly, or in castle grand.
And if, of those who take thee by the hand,
Some bid thee enter where the hearth is bare—
Where love is slain—where grief hath wrought de-
    spair,—
Thou too the lore of pain dost understand !
Thou too hast agonized when love was dead !
Where sorrow dwelleth, there dost thou belong !
Thou art not alien where a tear is shed !
So they who love and weep may heed thy song :
A song of sorrow not too sadly sung.
—What bard can sing, except his heart be wrung ?

THOU AND I:

A LYRIC OF HUMAN LIFE.

THOU AND I.

I.

" Thou and I!"
Cried he, an urchin gay ;
" Let us go forth to play,
Just we ourselves, we twain!"

Then, to the rock-bound main,
Along the billow-beaten strand,
Amid the flying spray,
He led her by her tiny hand,—
And, just above the water's reach,
They sat together on the beach,

And piled the shells and sand
Into a palace grand.
They built it like Aladdin's tower,—
Begun and finished in an hour.

The builders thought the building
A marvel to behold,
For fancy gave it gilding
More golden than of gold.

The Caliphs of the days of old
Had never such a royal court
As did those children in their sport.

" I now am king," cried he ;
" And I am queen," said she.

Then, over land and sea,
They held imperial sway,
One livelong day ;—

A happy day, whose sun
Went down on love begun
And twain made one !

II.

" THOU and I!"

Said he, in graver tone,—

Man-grown,—

Thick-bearded,—at her side;

A bridegroom by his bride;

The twain more royal than before,

Though king and queen no more.

Then, forth from the cathedral door,

They stepped on flowery ground,

And gazed around,—

From south to north,

From east to west,—

In sweet bewilderment profound

At which of all the roads seemed best,

Till, choosing one that led
They knew not where,
The never-parting pair,—
Brave man, fair wife,—
Began, with joint and jocund tread,
Their pilgrimage of life.

And though the path was never straight,
But ever winding,
And hard of finding,—
Yet on they went, with hearts elate ;
For Hope is not afraid of Fate.

"Dear love," said he, "the world is wide,
But howsoever wide it be,
It hath no land nor sea
To sunder thee and me :
So follow thou where I shall guide.

1*

" Beyond the mountains is a spot,—
A bosky dell,
With many a shepherd's lowly cot :
Arcadia, whereof poets tell :—

" A land where all is well ;
Where they who tarry sorrow not ;
Where happiness is each one's lot ;
Where heart from heart is never rent,
Nor faith betrayed
By man or maid,—
And lovers never love in vain ;

" For, in Arcadia's flowery plain,
Its ancient goddess, still divine,
Our Mother Mighty,
Great Aphrodité,
Hath willed that her unruined shrine
Forever shall remain ;
Which shepherdess and swain

Shall each new day entwine

With fresh red roses, and white lilies,

And yellow daffodillies,

And many a tangled eglantine,

And sacred ivy vine,—

To grace the holy fane;—

That so love's altar, ever newly decked,

May suffer no neglect,

And love may never wane;

" That never more, like sorrowing Clité,

Or jealous Amphitrité,

Or Ariadné by the main,

Shall any maiden pine

With love-sick pain,—

Nor sigh, through vigil long,

For love that came and went,—

Nor grieve at passion's false intent,—

Nor bear the world's disdain,

Nor self-reproach for wrong;—

"For there, once plighted at that altar,
Troth shall not fail nor falter,—
Love shall have nothing to repent,
Pride, nothing to resent,—
But golden days in peace be spent,
And silvery nights
Bring pure delights :—

"A land whose stilly air excludes
All loud alarm ;
Where, through the solemn solitudes,
A soft enchantment ever broods,
Beneath whose tranquil charm
No creatures lurk that hurt or harm ;—
No serpents in the grasses creep ;
No wolves prowl round the sheep ;
No hungry hawks molest
The pendulous, wind-blown nest
Wherein the oriole sways and swings ;
No scorpion stings ;

No thorn is rapier to the rose ;

No deadly nightshade grows,—

Nor that strange herb of Trebizond

Of which the bee, too fond,

Makes honey maddening to the brain ;

Nor that wild vine which Tamerlane

Sought out in Samarcand,—

Whose leaves, by noxious breezes fanned,

Grew lush with juices to anoint

His dagger's point,

That dealt a death with every blow ;

Nor, by the wayside, as we go,

Lurks any brier of poisonous bane

To prick, O love, thy soft white hand

While plucking blossoms through the land ;

Nor grows that gloomy tree of woe—

That fatal mistletoe—

Whose branches the Blind Thrower flings

(With death upon their wings)

At Balder, prince of kings,

To end his reign;

"Nor, in that pilgrim-trod domain,
Lies any wounding stone, O sweet,
To vex thy feet,—
Nor cutting flint, nor cruel shard;
But thou shalt softly pass—
On mosses, and lamb-nibbled grass—
Through shady glen, and leafy lane,
Where all the rocks, however hard,
Are piteous as when Edda's bard
Saw every pebble weep for Balder slain!

"And though in other lands, elsewhere,
The earth, that men call fair,
Hath even in its greenness
Some mildew, some uncleanness,—
Yet, in Arcadia's fairer zone,
No blasting blight is known;
Nor fades a flower that once hath blown;

Nor is there wilderness, nor waste,—

Like wild Sahara;

Nor font of bitter taste,—

Like Marah;

Nor bog Serbonian;

Nor *ignis fatuus* of the fen,

To tempt unwary men;

Nor vapor Acheronian;

Nor charnel odor foul;

Nor jackal's mournful howl;

Nor outcry of the owl;—

" But every meadow is as green

As that enameled turf, once seen

Ere yet Apollo ceased to rove

Through Daphné's grove;—

" And every fountain is as cool

As that unfathomable pool

Where Mimir, every morn,

Once lifted high his dripping horn;—

"And every murmur is as sweet

As when, by summer's heat,

The lute is mellowed and unstrung,—

Not sounding, only sighing;

Or when, in topmost flight,

Heard faintly, out of sight,

The lark sings, flying;

Or when, at dead of night,

Leaves rustle which the dews are sprinkling;

Or when Titania's bells

(The tiniest ever rung)

Are suddenly set tinkling

To call the fairies from afar

To Candahar.

"But, O sweet love, these words of mine

Are harsh and grating,

And fail in the relating

How those Arcadian notes combine,—

Now sinking, and now swelling,—
So clear, and yet so faint and fine
That the tale needeth, in the telling,
A voice as sweet as thine!

" For, in Arcadia's tuneful seat,
Each sound with which the air is stirred,
Each note, though warbled, hummed, or whirred,
Of singing bird,
Or buzzing bee,
Or the cicada on the tree,
Or cattle lowing,
Or wild wind blowing,—
All take their wondrous tunes
From those immortal runes
That first were heard,
And first were sung,
By Him who, when the world was young,
Nine days upon Ygdrasil hung,—

Self-wounded with his sacred spear,

To consecrate his listening ear

And hallow his intoning tongue.

"O bonny bride!—

In that rose-red retreat,—

In that Arcadian vale,—

There comes, as in Endymion's dale,

No snow, nor hail,

Nor rain, nor sleet,

Nor wind—except the wooing gale

That lulled, and lullabied,

And kissed Endymion till he died;

Or only feigned to die, instead,—

Too godlike to be dead,—

Asleep in love's sweet swoon, to wake

For pale Selené's sake,

Who watched above him, open-eyed:—

"A land that hath no winter's day,

But where the year is always May:—

And where, O love, the azure skies
Are blue as thy blue eyes,—
But not so tearless!—for, they say,
Those heavens, unwracked by thunderous storm,
Unswept by rainy wind,
Drip with bejeweled dews;
Outgleaming all the pearls of Orm,
Outflashing all the gems of Ind;
More rich than lover dares to choose
Wherewith to deck the maid he woos;
Each drop more crystal pure
Than wet the sandals of the Jews
On Hermon's dew-besprinkled hill,
Or than the chilly heavens distill
On Finland's frost-bespangled moor;
Nor do they vanish but endure;
At blazing noon they glitter still;
Not all the summer's fiery day
Can waste those deathless dews away;
Bestrewing the moist meads
With ever-sparkling beads,

That dry not as on Gideon's fleece;
For never càn their shining cease;
Their lustres they can never lose;—
Immortal as the dripping ooze
That trickles in each fabled fount
Of Helicon's twin-watered mount,—
Or as the drops that fill
Castalia's näiad-haunted rill,
Beloved of every muse:—

"A land of perfect peace;
For, as when Òrpheus smote his shell,
Wild beasts, though dabbled all with gore,
No longer one another tore,
But, to the strain entrancing
That set them dancing,
The lion did with leopard leap,
And did a concord keep,—
So, in that vale of asphodel,

Fierce men those furies quell

Which elsewhere through their bosoms sweep

With passion-panting swell,—

All tamed in that enchanting place

To gentle grace:—

"A land, dear heart, of heart's content ;

Where eyes, whose tears once fell,

Have not a woe to weep ;

Where neither murmur, nor lament,

Nor discord, nor dissent,

Nor sob, nor sigh

Disturbs the halcyon spell,—

But life and love are sweetly blent,

Harmonious as a marriage-bell !

"And, look ! the valley seems to lie,

Not distant, but near by,—

Where yonder white doves fly !

" So let us, thou and I,
Go thither and there dwell!"

—Then, starting ere the dews were dry,
When flowers are sweetest in their smell,
And hasting onward, blithe and gay,—
Albeit uncertain of the way,
But only toward Arcadia bent,—
The lovers thither wandering went
To pitch their tent.

III.

"THOU and I!"

Again to her quoth he.

"Come sit with me

Beneath this mulberry-tree,

And watch our children romp and play.

How wild they are, and gay!

How light and free!

O blessed is the children's glee!

Let them enjoy it while they may—

It cannot last—it will not stay!

Now, eager for the race,

They dash away,

With flying feet, and glowing face,

To leap and bound,

Like hare and hound,

And hunt each other round and round;

Now, weary of the chase,

The bonny band

All panting stand;

Now sit in circle on the ground;

And now, like busy elves,

Each digs and delves,

And builds of clay

A palace as we did ourselves,—

On that far-off and happy day

Beside the rock-bound sea!

" O thou and I, once young as they,

How now is life with thee and me?

" When first we started forth together,

The morning dews were on the heather;

But now the lark has done his tune;

The dial vergeth to the noon;

And, though we breast the breezy weather,
The midday sun fatigues us soon,—
Fatigues us more than when we crossed
Those mountains where our way we lost!
So let us rest a little now.

"I just discover on thy brow
An ornament so passing fair
That not the like did Venus wear,—
A single thread of silver hair;
As silvery as if finger-frayed
Or wind-plucked from Diana's braid;
Yea, silvery more than silver-bright,—
As if, at very zenith-height,
Apollo's chariot, in its flight,
Had crossed, at noon, the orb of night
And jarred its rays, and loosened down
Upon thy sunlit tresses brown
A moonbeam also for a crown!
    2

"O love, there is a rhyme that sings
How Time, with the keen scythe he swings,
Cuts down all living things;
But false is every fable
That vainly so pretends—
For Time is never able,
Though keen the blade he wieldeth,
To pierce what honor shieldeth,
Or wound what faith defends;
His powerful stroke
May fell the century oak,
But faithful love he cannot kill,
Assault it as he will.

"O tried and true!
There is a love that, soon or late,
Turns first to anger, then to hate,
Until the heart unmates its mate
And cuts.the cord in two.
But thou and I, who loved of yore,

Love on forever, as before,—
Not less and less, but more and more!

" So though we sought, but never found,
The fabled and enchanted ground
Where bloom Arcadia's happy bowers,
Behold what pleasant fruits and flowers
Grow in this garden here of ours!

" What fairer apples can there be
Than here fall golden from the tree?—
As round, and ripe, and splendid
As those Iduna watched and tended,—
Which, in that Hyperborean clime
Where gods grew old before their time,
The goddess, with her heavenly hand,
Fed to the hoary-bearded band
Till each regained his youth and prime.

" What purpler grapes have ever blushed

Than here hang waiting to be crushed?

As luscious are they in their look

As if they grew by Eschol's brook,

Or ripened red in serried ranks

On old Engeddi's terraced banks,

Or burst and bled

Beneath the tread

Of Judah's wine-press, flowing still

On ancient Zion's vine-clad hill,

Whose crimson clusters

Hold all the lustres

Of all the summer suns that shine

To flush the wine.

" What whiter lilies ever blow

Than here outgleam th' Iberian snow?

Or frosty wind-flower of the spring?

Or crested waves that whiten

When blown by trumpet of the Triton?

Or Jove's white wing

When he, a swan, in Leda's arms
Out-blanched their charms?

" What myrtles yield a sweeter bloom
Than thou and I have here entwined?—
None since that doleful day of doom
When, as Medina's maids relate,
The exiled Adam and his mate
Bore with them, out of Eden's gate,
A myrtle-flower, to keep in mind
The sweetness they had left behind.

" So, as for thee and me, what though,
As in the holy Hebrew tale,
The Nile forget to overflow,
And Egypt's harvests fail?
Yet still, of all our sunny fields,
Not one but yields
A laden wain
Of golden grain

To threshing-floor and flail !
For all the dews of night and morn
Are garnered in our corn,
And all the showers that come and pass
Are treasured in our grass.

" Let Famine, wan and pale,
Thin-visaged and forlorn,
Sit wasting where she will :
But here is Plenty's horn,
Which, as of old, so still
She empties but to fill,
And fills to empty, each in turn,
Until,
Like Neptune's urn,
Through which the endless rivers roared,
It ever full is stored,
Yet ever forth is poured,
With ever-emptying, never-emptied hoard.

" So, for the abundance on our board,

We praise the Lord !

" Or, if the skies bring hurricanes,

And oak and vine uprooted lie,

And harvests mildew in the rains,

And fig and olive fail and die,—

Who is it murmurs or complains?

It is not thou—it is not I.

For God who takes, like God who gives,

Is God the same—

All glory to His name !

So if He gives, or if He takes,

It still is for our sakes.

" From the high Heaven in which He lives,

To the low earth on which He reigns,

He to the sons of men ordains

That ills (as mortals call them)

Shall evermore befall them !

" Forecast in God's eternal plan

Are good and evil unto man,—

No less of evil than of good :

Strange mystery, never understood !

But if the wind that bloweth

So cometh and so goeth

That whence or whither no man knoweth,—

Who then shall understand

The counsel dark, the purpose dim,

And all the secret ways of Him

Who holds the winds within His hand?

"Of all the gifts that Heaven bestoweth,

The rod of God's affliction

Is man's best benediction.

" If first there cometh laughter—

Or jest—or jubilation,—

Then, swiftly after,

God sendeth lamentation !

" Good is not good, if single ;

So good and evil intermingle.

The gold hath need of the alloy.

Is Heaven a place of perfect joy ?

Not if, of joys, it lacks the chief—

The joy of grief.

" Had Heaven to such an earth as this

Decreed a perfect bliss,

Then men, unmanned by such a scheme,

Would say, ' Now we may doze and dream,

Or take our ease in idle state,

And indolently wait

While bounteous Heaven itself fulfilleth

Our happy fate.'

" Instead whereof, God willeth

That man shall labor, long and late,—

With struggle, sweat, and groan ;

For not a field he tilleth

Is his to reap except as he hath sown.

2*

"The world is full of woe and sin :
Fresh griefs invade it day by day.
How dare they thus intrude therein ?
By what strange warrant tarry they ?
Could mortal miseries come or stay,
Were Heaven to will them once away ?
If God be God, and none but He,
Then how, against His high decree,
Could such things be ?
Or how, upon the cassia-tree,
Could cankers grow ?
Or locusts gnaw the lily-leaf ?
Or rotting rust
Despoil the harvest-sheaf
While hunger crieth for a crust ?
Or human bosoms burn with lust ?
Or plague stalk to and fro ?
Or graves be dug, and hearts laid low ?

" Men little know,

While they to Heaven are suing

For all the blessings of the blest,

That oft the miseries they are ruing

Are God's own doing,

Who knoweth best.

The Judge of all the earth is just:

Then all His judgments, too, are so.

Whatever drops of sorrow flow,

Or spear into the soul is thrust,

Or fiery bolt the bosom sears

With heat unquenchable by tears,—

Whatever may befall,

God's love is in it all.

" Now it is Heaven's behest,

That every heaving human breast,

Instead of finding rest,

Shall thrill with joys—shall throb with aches—

Until it glows—until it breaks ;—

That good and ill—that weal and woe—
Like equal forces, foe to foe—
Shall in the bosom strive and strain,
Each its own empire to maintain,
Till, wearied, panting, out of breath,
The fainting heart at last shall feel,—
Whichever triumphs, woe or weal,—
Be fortune high, or fortune low,
It matters not how goes the strife,
Since Love, and Love alone, is life!
' For I am fickle,' Fortune saith,—
But Love is faithful unto death.

" In all our losses, all our gains,
In all our pleasures, all our pains,
The life of life is,—Love remains.

" In every change from good to ill,—
If love continue still,
Let happen then what will.

"Come wildest storm that ever burst!

Let the tornado blow!

Come crash and overthrow!

Let fate, accurst,

Fulfill its worst,—

Heaven's bolt without Heaven's bow!

Be all our treasures scattered wide,—

Till joy, and pride,

And hope, and all beside

Be to the wild winds strown,—

All tempest-blown

To coasts unknown,—

All swept beyond recall,—

All, all save love alone,—

Yet love alone is all in all!

"If love abide,

If love endure,—

Strong through its sufferings borne,

And, through its sorrows, pure,—

Then, whatsoever test
Prove other precious things unsure ;
Whatever cup of pleasure—
Filled high to over-measure—
Be spilled and wasted
Ere it be tasted ;
Whatever plume the Fates have shorn
From Fortune's crest ;
Whatever losses men may mourn ;
Whatever be the prize—the treasure
Whereof the soul is dispossessed ;—
Whoso hath love can lose the rest
And still be blest !

" Love, homeless and forlorn ;
Love, beggared, tattered, torn ;
Love, robbed by fate
Of all its fair estate
Till nought remains its own ;—
No pillow for its head
Except a stone,—

Whereon, from night till morn,

Its temples beat

With fever heat;

No sandals for its feet,—

Till, naked to the thorn,

The trail they tread

Is tinged at last blood-red;

No pilgrim's scallop-shell,

Nor wayside well

Wherein to dip

To cool its parching lip;

No wild bees' honey sweet,

But only bitter bread to eat,

With wine of gall;—

"Love, even so distraught,

So stripped of all things, so bereft

That only its own self is left,—

Love, perfect still,

And fearing nought,

Though losing all,—

Love, love,—which no despair can kill,

Nor misery can appal,—

From its deep depths of woe shall call,

And shall of Heaven a boon implore;

And what shall be Love's prayer?

No plea of empty palms

For beggar's alms!—

No golden dross

For recompense of loss!—

No sheltering hut nor hall!—

No heritage, how great or small!—

No stock, nor store!—

Nor aught of all it had before,

In happier days of yore,

Save only its old touch and thrill

To work its wondrous will,

And knit two hearts together still,

Twain one forevermore!

" O winsome wife, we know,—

The further into life we go,—

There is no power on earth below,

No power in Heaven above,

No power of all the powers of hell,

Where all the powerful passions dwell,—

No power to do, no power to bear,

In bliss, in anguish, in despair,

In everything and everywhere,—

No power omnipotent as love !

" O marvellous was the might sublime

That mighty minstrels chanted of,

In many a high heroic rhyme,

Of giants of the olden time !—

" They sang how, all distained with grime,

Each panting Argonaut,

When home the Golden Fleece was brought,—

In sweaty phalanx, all as one,

On many groaning shoulders bore
Their huge ship up the shore.

" They sang how writhingly were wrought
The twelve great toils,—
The weariest ever done
Beneath th' unpitying sun.

" They sang how fuming was the fret
Of him who, in the viewless net,
Against the unseen coils—
(More filmy than the spider's woof,
And yet more fracture-proof
Than brazen chain)—
Tugged, godlike, yet in vain.

" They sang how sinewy was the strain
Of him who evermore uprolled
Th' enchanted stone that slipped his hold
And bounded back from hill to plain
To be upheaved again with might and main.

" Yea, many a song they sang beside,

How the all-valiant gods, in pride,

With one another vied ;—

" How naked Vulcan, clad with smoke,

His ringing anvil beat

Until his hammer's heat,

With just its spark-enkindling stroke,

Struck fiercer fire at every blow

Than in his forge could ever glow ;

How Jove in wrath the Titans hurled,

Down whizzing to the lower world ;

How Ossa was on Pelion flung ;

How Arthur's sword was three times swung ;

How Charlemagne's battle-brand,—

Which he alone could hold,—

Too ponderous for another's hand,—

Flashed lightnings through the land ;

How Lion Heart in fury fought

With Saladin the bold ;—

"The minstrels sang, and sang again,
Of mighty gods, of mighty men,
Of giants in the days of old,
Of heroes of immortal mould,
Till all the earth with echoes rang,—
So well they sang!

"But all this marvellous might was nought,
In act or thought,
Compared with Love, when comes the hour
To prove its more than mortal power!

"Though all the Fates should be its foes,
And smite it all the blows
That rained on Hector's helmet,
They could not overwhelm it!

"O Earth! O Heaven! Behold!
Of all the powers that are, or seem,
In fact or dream,
Love is supreme!

" No mortal breath,

No lip that uttereth speech or song.

No word that any poet saith,

No urn or marble after death,

No art, however long,

No tongue of time hath ever told

The might of love, how manifold,—

The strength of love, how strong !

" Love, strong as Samson at the gates,—

Love, stronger than the Triple Fates,—

Love, strongest of the strong,—in patience
        waits,

Like Atlas, long,—until at length,

With mighty load, yet mightier strength,

It heaves the dusty world on high

And holds it in the breezy sky

For Heaven's own winds to purify !

"Love, fiercer far

Than blazing flame of sun or star,

Is that immortal fire,

The soul's supreme desire,

Th' eternal heat

That gives the heart its perfect beat,

And maketh life complete.

" So thou and I, my sweet,

Sit at love's feet!"

—The matron listened, glowed, and smiled;

Then caught and kissed each romping child.

IV.

" THOU and I !"

The old man said,—fourscore,

Snow-crowned, and form erect no more.

" Let us to Him whom we adore

Give thanks and praise,

For He who lengtheneth out our days

Hath given us twain our mortal measure

Of all the needful toil and strife—

Of all the needful peace and pleasure—

Which they who live call life.

" Our stalwart sons are scattered far,—

All following fortune's flying star,

That leads the brave where honors are.

"Our gentler birds have softlier flown,

Each with her mate through tranquil skies,

Each to her nest in quiet shades,

Till now, of all those mated maids,

Each daughter is a matron grown,

Each mothering daughters of her own.

"The heart alone

Is woman's throne,—

A shaken throne of hopes and fears,

Yet, as among the twinkling spheres

The star, most fixt, most trembles,—lo!

A woman's heart is even so:

The more it quivers in her breast,

The deeper its foundations rest!

"What honors shall a woman prize?

In love, her queenly glory lies,—

Till in her children's princely eyes,

And in their father's kingly worth,
She sums the Empire of the Earth.

" But now, to thee and me,
What more of honor can there be?
What laurel-wreath, what garland grand
Was ever snatched by palsied hand?

" For us, the almond-tree
Doth flourish now:
Its whitest bloom is on our brow.
Let others triumph as they may,
And wear their garlands gay
Of olive, oak, or bay:
Our crown of glory is, instead,
The hoary head.

" Our threescore years and ten,
That measure life to mortal men,
Have lingered to a longer length
By reason of our strength;

3

Yet, like a tale that hath been told,
They all have passed, and now, behold!
We verily are old ;—

" Yea, old like Abraham, when he went,
With head down bent,
And mantle rent,
In dole for her who lay in death,
And to the Sons of Heth
The silver shekels gave
For Mamré's gloomy cave,
To be her grave ;—

" Or, older still, like him
Who, feeble not of limb,
With eyes not dim,
Upclimbed, with staff in hand,
To where Mount Nebo cleft the sky,
And looked and saw the Promised Land
(Forbidden him from on high)

Till, with an unrecorded cry,
He laid him down to die.

" So too, for us, the end is nigh.
Our mortal race is nearly run ;
Our earthly toil is nearly done !
Ah, thou and I,
Who in the grave so soon shall lie,
Have little time to see the sun—
So little it is nearly none !

" What then ?
Amen !
All hail, my love, good cheer !
Keep back thy unshed tear !
Not thou nor I
Shall mourn or sigh.
Nay now, we twain—
Old man, old wife—
The few days that remain—

Let us make merry—let us laugh !—

For now at length we quaff

The last, best wine of life,—

The very last—the very best,

The double cup of love and rest !

" What though the groaning world declare

That life is but a load of care ?—

A burden wearisome to bear ?—

That as we journey down the years

The path is through a vale of tears ?—

Yet we who have the burden borne,

And traveled until travel-worn,

Forget the weight upon the back,

Forget the long and weary track,

And sit remembering here to-day

How we were children at our play ;—

" And, half in doze, at idle ease,

Before the hearth-fire's dying brands,

With elbows on our trembling knees,

With chin between our wrinkled hands,

We sail unnavigable seas,—

We roam impenetrable lands,—

We leap from clime to clime,—

We conquer space and time;—

" For, every glowing ember

Enkindles fancy to remember,—

Till all the once-forgotten past,

Long gone, comes back to us at last;—

As if the sea should render up,

From out its treasure-hiding caves,

The King of Thulé's golden cup;

Or the green Adriatic's waves

Back to the wondering Doge should fling

Venetia's bridal-ring;

Or Ghizeh's time-defying graves

Should burst their marble lids asunder,

And, to the Bedouin's wonder,

Reveal th' Egyptian jewels, hid
By that sphinx-guarded pyramid
Which they are buried under!

" And, howsoever strange it seems,
The dearest of our drowsy dreams
Is of that billow-beaten shore
Where, in our childish days of yore,
We piled the salty sands
Into a palace that still stands !—
Not where it first arose,
Not where the wild wind blows,
Not by the ocean's roar,—
(For, long ago, those turrets fell
Beneath that billowy swell),—
But, down within the heart's deep core,
Our tumbled tower we oft restore
And ever build it o'er and o'er!

" We have one palace more,—
Not made with hands,—

Nor have our feet yet entered at its door!
It lieth not behind us, but before!

" Dear love, our pilgrimage is thither tending,
And there shall have its ending!

" At first, we sought, like all mankind,
The land that all have failed to find,—
Arcadia, by the poets sung,—
That pleasant phantom of the mind
That lured our feet when we were young ;

" At last, with souls no longer haunted
By that vain vision, soon forgot,
We seek,—not that Utopia fair
That vanished into viewless air,—
Not that all-rosy realm which, like the flowery
　　　　spot
Where Eden's garden once was planted,
No longer is enchanted,

And bloometh not;—
We seek,—with unmisguided feet,
And hearts undaunted,—
Not hope's mirage, not fancy's cheat,
Not faith's fair fabulous pretence,
Not any phantom to beguile
The spirit for a while,
Then disappoint the sense ;—
We seek,—not on the mocking earth, not here,
(Yet, haply, not far hence)—
The Heavenly City, crystal clear !—
Which, lustrous with a light intense,
Was seen from Patmos by the Seer
Whose century-old and dazzled eyes
Beheld it shining in the skies !—

" No vision, for a moment bright,
Then taking flight !
But its huge bulk was measured to his sight,
As he hath told,

By an archangel's reed of gold ;

Length, breadth, and height,

Each equaling each,

Whichever way the reed could reach,—

Each several side twelve thousand furlongs

    square,—

All glittering in the upper air!—

So lustrous long, so flashing high,

So blazing broad, no mortal eye

Hath space within its ball

To compass all

The golden girth

Of that translucent wall,

Outmeasuring every mountain on the earth !

" For neither Himmaláya's crest,

Where the tired eagle stops to rest ;

Nor Hecla's burning pile,

Whose smoke rolls up for many a lofty mile ;

Nor Tenerif's cloud-confronting isle ;

    3*

Nor the five Cities of the Plain;

Nor that engulphing main

Wherein their shaken towers, in falling,

Sank in th' asphaltic flood, appalling;—

Not all these mountains, cities, seas,—

Though heaped in one,—nor seven times these!—

Could measure forth the space

Of God's great dwelling-place;—

That City of Delight,

Fixt in Heaven's highest height—

Unsunned, unmooned,

Yet needing not the ray

Of any orb that gilds the day,

Or beautifies the night;

Untempled, yet attuned

To praise divine,

For they who worship there need not a shrine,

Since they behold His face.

" To thee, O love, will I repeat

The sacred story

That tells that City's glory !—

" For there, through many a golden street,

Th' Immortal River floweth,

Upon whose banks there groweth—

On either side—

The Tree of Life, whose branches midway meet

To overarch the amber tide,

That pictures all their pendent fruits

Deep in the glassy flood that glides along their

　　　roots ;

And ever as the waveless stream goes wending

Its tranquil way,

It watereth plants that need no other tending,

Self-tended they ;—

And, chief, that amaranthine flower, transplanted

　　　first

From Heaven to Eden's garden,

To bloom awhile ere man was yet accurst,

But then, on his offending,

And while his punishment was pending,

In heavenly token of his pardon,

Plucked back again, above earth's death and doom,

To where, beyond the tomb,

It purples with a fadeless bloom

A spring unending,—

To crown victorious souls, on their ascending,

With that immortal wreath for which they died

    contending.

" And each of all the twelve great portals

Is one great pearl,—

Gold-banded, like a ring of fair device ;

With adamantine hinges, ever-during ;

Each pearl with lustre so alluring

That though beyond the gaze of mortals,—

Above the earth's wild whirl,—

Yet from afar it sweetly doth entice

The souls of men to wish them in that Paradise ;

Each pearl of greater price

Than in the parable is told

Of him who all his treasures sold,

His silver and his gold,

And went and bought with these

That jewel of the seas,—

That gem, all precious, pure, and rare,

With which none others could compare—

Except the pearls those portals hold,

Ten thousand times more fair!

" And at each portal an archangel waits

To keep wide open those eternal gates ;

For he who saw was bid to say,

' The gates shall not be shut by day,

And there is no night there.'

" And each foundation glittereth fair

With heavenly stones, half-dimmed with earthly
	names,

As if to veil from mortal eyes their flames,

Lest their unshaded brightness should excel

All power of tongue to tell,—

Or lest, with eyes transpierced with pain,

The Holy Seer had fallen blind,—

Whereby, beheld too plain,

The vision, unrecorded to mankind,

Had come and passed in vain.

"And those illustrious stones—the mystic twelve—

Each for a tribe of Israel's line—

More fiercely shine

Than any for which mortals delve

In any earthly mine!—

" For not Golconda nor Brazil,

In cavern dark, or deep-dug hill,

Illumes the slave's dim-lighted glance

With that fair spark which happy chance

Unblinds his searching eyes to see,

And, for his finding, sets him free ;—

Not this soul-ransoming gem,

Nor Cæsar's glittering diadem

Hath power to burn, and blaze,

And charm th' enchanted gaze

Like those fair jewels in the rays

Of that immortal light

Of which the mortal eye bears not the sight,

But whose white glory the Archangels praise.

" O love, now lend thine ear and listen

While, like the Patmian, I declare

How those twelve jewels glisten,

And what the names they bear.

" The first, a jasper,—which in Ispahan,

When brought by camel of the caravan,

Is called a diamond in the speech of man;

The next, a sapphire,—whose celestial blue

Gives the Tyrrhenian waves their hue;

The third, that Chalcedonian stone
Which men no longer find,
Yet once on earth was known
In that old City of the Blind
Which dust of deserts since hath overblown;
The fourth, an emerald,—glittering green
As when, upon an olive's rind,
A drop of dew is seen;
The fifth, a sard,—that stone of flesh
That ever bleeds afresh,
And stands for Calvary's blood-red sign;
The sixth, a ruby,—set to shine
Like th' ensanguined wine
That filled the Holy Grail;
The seventh, a chrysolite,—
So golden bright
It makes Aurora dim and pale;
The eighth, a beryl,—sparkling white,
Like moonlit frost,

As seen by hunters who, at night,

Mount Caucasus have crossed;

The ninth, a topaz,—hazel-eyed

Like Lilith, Adam's earlier bride

Whom first he loved and lost

Ere Eve was moulded from his side;

The tenth, a chrysoprase,—

Flashing, with yellow rays,

Up, down, a thousand ways,

Through all that region wide;

Th' eleventh, a jacinth,—fairer than if dyed

By sun and wind

With colors of that blossom, lush and pied,

With which its name is twinned;

The last, an amethyst,—whose font of fire

Casts forth a purple jet

More orient than the East,—

As if the day should rise but not to set,

And the red dawn, with all its gay adorning,

Should linger on in one immortal morning!

" O fair that City is to see
That lureth thee and me!
It is arrayed in bride's attire!
It celebrates the marriage-feast!
It satisfies the soul's desire!
With strength declined, yet faith increased,
We thitherward aspire!

" As he whose way, through briers and weeds,
To royal Shiraz leads
(Where the rose-gardens are),
May guess his nearness, from afar,
As soon as he espies
With gladdened eyes
That towering, that enchanted tree
Which, never by a zephyr stirred,
Nor rustled by a fluttering bird,
Yet, by its own sweet action free,
Waves in that breathless air of balm,
And, in a perfect calm,

Bends its high top in courtesy,
And, with a gracious nod,
Salutes each passing pilgrim-band
To bid them welcome to the land ;—
So, in the Paradise of God,
The Tree of Life, with greener plume,
Unearthly in its bloom,
Already waves its signal-bough,
And, like a beckoning hand,
Which we, beholding, understand,
Invites us thither now!

" To which celestial welcome, what reply
Make thou and I?

" Ah, though the rapturous vision
Allures us to a Land Elysian,
Yet aged are our feet, and slow,
And not in haste to go.

" Life still hath many joys to give,
Whereof the sweetest is—to live.

" Then fear we death ?   Not so!
Or do we tremble ?   No !
Nor do we even grieve !
And yet a gentle sigh we heave,
And unto Him who fixes fate,—
Without whose sovereign leave,
Down-whispered from on high,
Not even the daisy dares to die,—
We, jointly, thou and I,
Implore a little longer date,—
A little term of kind reprieve,—
A little lease till by and by !

" May it be Heaven's decree,—
Here, now, to thee and me,—
That, for a season still,
The eye shall not grow dim ;

That, for a few more days,

The ear cease not to hear the hymn

Which the tongue utters to His praise;

That, for a little while,

The heart faint not, nor fail;

For even the wintry sun is bright,

And cheering to our aged sight;

Yea, though the frosts prevail,

Yet even the icy air,

The frozen plain, the leafless wood

Still keep the earth as fresh and fair

As when from Heaven He called it good!

"O final Summoner of the soul!

Grant, of thy pitying grace,

That, for a little longer space,

The pitcher at the fountain's rim

Be shattered not, but still kept whole,—

Still overflowing at the brim!

If but a year, if but a day,
Thy lifted hand, O stay!
Loose Thou not yet, O Lord,
The silver cord!
Break Thou not yet the golden bowl!"

—Thus, garrulous, the aged pair
Sat in their chimney-nook,
With hearts half glad and half afraid;
And while the firelight flickered there,
They talked and laughed—they wept and prayed;
Until, with weary, wistful look,
They saw the embers fade,—
And, darkly through the wintry air,
Came nightfall and the shade!

V.

"THOU and I!"

The voice no longer said ;

But two white stones, instead,

Above the twain, long dead,

Still utter, each to each,

The same familiar speech,

" Thou and I!"—

Not spoken to the passer-by,

But just as if, beneath the grass,

Deep underfoot of all who pass,

The sleeping dust should wake to say,

Each to its fellow-clay,

Each in the same old way,

"Thou and I!"

And each to either should reply,—
(Tomb murmuring unto tomb,
Stone answering unto stone,
Yet not with sound of human moan,
Nor breath of mortal sigh,
But voiceless as the dead's dumb cry,)—
" Thou and I ! "

And whosoever draweth nigh,—
With reverent feet and holy fear,—
And tarrieth for a space,
The letters on the stones to trace,
Or drop a tender tear,
Shall (if he have an ear to hear,
And know the language of the place,)
Hear other whisperings to and fro,
Half-muffled in the dust below;
Not said in words, nor sounded clear,
But, though all mystic to the ear,

Yet to the heart all plain;—

A silent speech by sign and token,

More sweet than any language spoken;—

At first, the old refrain,

" Thou and I ! "

Then, by and by,

This faintly added strain :—

" We twain,

As here we rest within the gloom,

Are sundered not, but still remain

Twain one,

As when we walked beneath the sun!

Love, lying in the grave—its bed—

Is not unwed,

But newly-nuptialed—groom and bride

Forever side by side—

As if the faithful dead

Had never died!

4

"The spirit and the body part,

Yet love abideth, heart to heart.

"O silent comrade of my rest,

With hands here crossed upon thy breast,

I know thee who thou art !

O marble brow,

Here pillowed next to mine,

I know the soul divine

That tenanted thy shrine !

"For, though above us, green and high,

The yew-trees grow,

And churchyard ravens fly,

And mourners come and go,

Yet thou and I,

Who dust to dust lie here below,

Still one another know !

" Yea, thee I know—it still is thou ;
And me thou know'st—it still is I ;
True lovers once, true lovers now !—
The same old vow,
The same old thrill,
The same old love between us still !

" The gloomy grave hath frosts that kill,
But love is chilled not with their chill.

" Love's flame —
Consuming, unconsumed—
In breasts that breathe—in hearts entombed—
Is fed by life and death the same !

" Love's spark
Is brightest when love's house is dark !

" Love's shroud—
That wraps its bosom round—
Must crumble in the charnel-ground,

Till all the long white winding-sheet
Shall drop to dust from head to feet;
But love's strong cord,
Th' eternal tie,
Th' immortal bond that binds
Love's twain immortal minds;—
This silken knot
Shall never rot—
Nor moulder in the mouldy mound—
Nor mildew—nor decay—
Nor fall apart—nor drop away—
Nor ever be unbound!

" Love's dust,
Whatever grave it fill,
Though buried deep, is deathless still!
Love hath no death, and cannot die!
This love is ours, as here we lie,—
Thou and I!"

THE CHANT CELESTIAL.

THE CHANT CELESTIAL.

I.

KING ARTHUR, in his palace of Pendragon,

Sat feasting with his princes, late and long,

And to his oldest minstrel sent a flagon

To fire his aged fancy to a song.

II.

Uprose the hoary harper, blind and saintly,

Whose   ninety-wintered   beard   besnowed   his

breast,

Who, harping with his palsied fingers faintly,

Thus sang, though softly, at the king's behest:

III.

" Give ear, whoever sorrows or rejoices,
    While I, too old for either mirth or tears,
Shall rhyme of those celestial harps and voices
    That chant the fabled music of the spheres.

IV.

" I sing of worlds before the earth was present,—
    A song of times ere time itself began,—
Before the silvery moon had lit her crescent,
    Or sun his fire, or lived a mortal man.

V.

" The primal universe had chaos in it,
    For night with triple darkness wrapped it round,
Nor was there greening leaf, nor singing linnet,
    Nor any other cheering sight, nor sound.

VI.

" Then, while the mighty mists were still concealing
  The sphereless world (not yet an asteroid),
God ordered heavenly music to go pealing
  Through all the silence of the earthly void.

VII.

" Within a shining cloud, that veiled their faces,
  Ten thousand seraphs, each with harp in hand,
Flew chanting through the still and empty spaces
  . That afterward were filled with sea and land.

VIII.

" The stars, that on the morning of creation
  Together sang to Him who made them fair,
First caught their canticle of adoration
  From this immortal murmur in the air.
    4*

IX.

" Before the mountains had their high upheaval,
Before the caverns of the deep were laid,
This was creation's harmony primeval,—
The rhythm to which the whirling world was
made.

X.

" Sweet herald of the will of the Creator,
It timed the birth of Nature, then unborn,
And, warbling through the zodiac and equator,
Awoke the seasons and led forth the morn.

XI.

" From pole to pole, from Capricorn to Cancer,
Things lifeless into life it did beguile,
Till marble-Memnon heard it and made answer,
And stony Sphinx retold it to the Nile.

XII.

" Swift in its flight, this cloud of glory glistened
  With lustre fairer than the sun or moon ;
And to its anthem, hill and valley listened
  Till earth, enchanted, echoed back the tune.

XIII.

" The rustling boughs of Lebanon, gigantic,
  Rehearsed it to the tiniest herbs that grew ;
And from the swelling wave of the Atlantic,
  It quavered to the trembling drop of dew.

XIV.

" Th' Almighty, who decreed this Chant Celestial,
  By its primordial melody designed
To chord to it all cadences terrestrial,
  As this was chorded to th' Eternal Mind.

XV.

" Awhile, through all the world, in each direction,
No earthly sound could ever sink or swell
But to that heavenly rhythm,whose lost perfection
Now lingers only in the sea-side shell.

XVI.

" The perfect earth kept not its first completeness,
But rolled in discord to the heavenly hymn,
Yet not the forfeiture of Eden's sweetness
Could hush the anthem of the cherubim.

XVII.

" They chant it in a flying cloud forever,
Yet not a cloud of earth, that caps the hills,
Nor yet of heaven—where cloud can enter never—
But midway where unfallen dew distils.

XVIII.

" This cloud by other clouds is unattended,
But floats in golden light above them all,
Yet hides from mortal eyes its glory splendid,
Though oft on mortal ears its echoes fall.

XIX.

" A whirlwind rose, and tore its flying fleeces,
And cleft its fleeting music to the core,—
Till now each earthly storm that roars or ceases
Is keyed to that celestial strain of yore.

XX.

" A soaring lark, that heard the heavenly singing,
Brought down the song to all his fellow-throats,—
Till every greenwood now is ever ringing
With lowly pipings of those lofty notes.

XXI.

" Beneath a myrtle sat a poet, sighing,
    Because he could not tune his jangled lyre,
Who heard the wondrous chant above him flying,
    And chorded to it each rebellious wire.

XXII.

" Then, having caught the arch-angelic measure,
    Henceforth, at wedding-feast and funeral-train,
He shed a heavenly joy on earthly pleasure,
    And cast a heavenly peace on earthly pain.

XXIII.

" When, round the ark, the Deluge rose, appalling,
    From this melodious cloud a lyre was hurled,
Whose seven immortal strings took fire in falling,
    And gave the rainbow to a stormy world.

XXIV.

"So lucent was the cloud, the sky adorning,
  That, when it crossed Olympus on its way,
It lent Aurora light to flush the morning,
  And gave Apollo gold to gild the day.

XXV.

"It flashed the sparkle which the moon saw
    glancing
  Upon the waters of Castalia's fount,
And lent the Muses music for their dancing
  Until they vanished from their vernal mount.

XXVI.

"It gleamed where Arctic islands caught its
    dazzle,—
  While rumbling icebergs echoed back its runes,
Till Odin heard them on the tree Ygdrasil,
  And bees re-hummed them to the summer
    noons.

XXVII.

" From India's sacred coast of Coromandel
    To Mecca's first Kaába went the sound,
Till he who listened laid aside his sandal,
    And flung him prostrate on the holy ground.

XXVIII.

" It blew a trumpet over Sinai's mountain,
    That woke an earthquake by its awful tone,
Till he who smote the rock and loosed the foun-
        tain
    Received the tables twain of graven stone.

XXIX.

" It sounded through the desert its hosanna
    Where, first beheld of men, a Pillar vast,
It shone before the tribes that gathered manna,
    And led them to the Promised Land at last.

XXX.

" Its harps were echoed by the harp of Zion,
   That prophesied of nations reconciled,
And of the peaceful day when lamb and lion
   Shall twain be yoked together by a child.

XXXI.

" The shepherds heard it, who by night were
      tending
   Their sleepy sheep on Bethlehem's holy hill,
To whose low summit came the cloud descending,
   With all its angels, chanting, ' Peace—good
      will ! '

XXXII.

" This was the cloud beneath whose pealing thun-
      ders
   The Temple reeled, the tombs flew open wide,
And all the day grew dark with signs and wonders
   When Calvary's Cross upbore the Crucified ! "

XXXIII.

[Here paused the bard ; and, at the Name All Holy,
  The king and princes, to the King of Kings,
Each crossed his breast, and bowed in reverence
    lowly,—
  The bard the lowliest,—and resumed the strings:]

XXXIV.

" In elder time, from out this cloud supernal, .
  Those guilty seraphs who did Heaven assault
Were headlong plunged to the abyss infernal,
  And discord vanished out of Heaven's blue vault.

XXXV.

" But discord on the earth is ever raging,
  For human hate is quenchless in its flame,
Yet, high above the wars that men are waging,
  The angels still go singing, all the same.

XXXVI.

" Above the bedlam world, but never near it,
　　Their floating chant is caroled through the sky,
So faint and far that mortals hardly hear it,
　　Yet he who hearkens hears it by and by.

XXXVII.

" It smites the ear with such a soft vibration
　　That some who hear it think it not a sound,
But fancy it their spirit's own pulsation,
　　That thrills the sense with ecstasy profound.

XXXVIII.

" It chimes to deserts and dim wildernesses,
　　In swift pursuit where wandering feet have trod;
And whom it overtakes, it sweetly blesses,—
　　And fills the pilgrim with the peace of God.

XXXIX.

" It chanteth to the sailor on the ocean,

    And in the tempest gives his soul a calm ;

It seeks the hermit, rapt in his devotion,

    And thrills and trembles in his prayer and psalm.

XL.

" Beyond all melody of pipe or tabor

    When merry maidens dance with happy men,

It glads the groaning captive at his labor,

    And cheers the exile, hunted to his den.

XLI.

" To all who weep at bedsides of the dying,

    To all who kiss their dead and lay them low,

To all the sorrowing world, with all its sighing,—

    It chants a solace greater than the woe.

XLII.

" The Heaven of heavens where God hath fixt His
    dwelling,
  Where, in the highest, reigneth the Most High,
Hath not, in all its heights, a hymn excelling
  This earth-encircling chorus in the sky.

XLIII.

" From Heaven to earth its cadences shall quiver,
  Till earthly lust shall yield to heavenly law ;
For so the oracles of God deliver,
  And so, of old, th' anointed seers foresaw.

XLIV.

" O anthem which the hymns of Heaven resemble !
  O harp with which no strings on earth compare !
From upper skies, that with thy rapture tremble,
  Float down to ravish now our lower air !

XLV.

" O cloud-wrapped cloud, hid in the heights Ely-
    sian,
  If waking eyes may not behold thy gleams,
Let loose thy angels, as in Jacob's vision,
  To steal upon our sleeping world in dreams !

XLVI.

" Shine once again, as over Eden's garden !
  Give back the later world its elder light !—
Till man no longer hath a sin to pardon !—
  Till earth no longer hath a wrong to right !

XLVII.

" Be chariot thou of Him of hallowed story !—
  Of Him foretold by all the holy seers !—
Of Him who cometh in a cloud of glory
  To reign upon the earth a thousand years !

XLVIII.

' O far-off harbinger of *His* appearing
  For whom men cry, 'How long, O God, how
    long!'—
I see, though blind, a vision of thy nearing!—
  I hail thee, harp for harp, and song for song!"

XLIX.

—So sang the minstrel till his strength was ended;
  And when his song was done, he gasped for
    breath—
Uprolled his eyes to heaven—his palms extended—
  And sank, through holy prayer, to happy death.

L.

King Arthur bade the princes of his table
  Uplift and lay thereon the fallen seer,
And on his bosom spread a pall of sable,—
  Till, black amid the banquet, was a bier.

LI.

Not mortal, like the bard,—his song, undying,

    Survives the singer and his crumbled lyre,—

For, round the listening earth, forever flying,

    God's holy angels chant it with their choir!

THE GRAVE ON THE PRAIRIE.

THE GRAVE ON THE PRAIRIE.

I.

I GALLOPED once with horse and hound,
  Across the Texan prairie,
Till, on a gentle swell of ground,
I halted by a flowery mound
  That bore the name of Mary.

II.

It was not where the living dwelt,
  Nor was it yet God's Acre,
But all a lonely, boundless belt,
Where she whose name the letters spelt
  Dwelt only with her Maker.

III.

No crumbling wall, nor rotting rail,
  Nor palisade of osier
Remained to show, however frail,
It once had girt the sacred pale,
  Or guarded the enclosure.

IV.

No date was carved of death or birth,
  No line of love or honor,
No tribute to departed worth,—
Yet she who mouldered, earth to earth,
  Had all earth's pomp upon her:

V.

For prairie-flowers, through many a mile,
  In every gay direction,
Were stirred of breezes all the while,
And caught the sun, and flashed his smile,
  And twinkled in reflection.

VI.

The fiery orb was zenith high,
    And yet the spot was shaded,
Because a live-oak grew hard by,
And arched it from the burning sky,
    And kept the flowers unfaded.

VII.

And long, gray moss, with mournful grace,
    Each lofty limb festooning,
Hung drooping round the pensive place,—
Where, tarrying from the morning chase,
    I took an hour of nooning.

VIII.

The hounds, all panting from their quest,
    I leashed with easy fetter,
And sat me by the dead to rest,—
For not so good is life, at best,
    But that the grave is better.

IX.

Then, while the bison joined his herd,
    In peace from my pursuing,
I watched the mosses as they stirred,
And listened to the whispered word
    Of what the winds were doing.

X.

The frightened plover whirred his wing;
    The startled rabbit bounded;
And not a bird made bold to sing;
Nor in the grass a creeping thing
    His chirping trumpet sounded.

XI.

The cactus flaunted, far and near,
    His blossom red and splendid,
Which nibbling sheep approached with fear,
Half daunted by the spiny spear
    With which it was defended.

XII.

No wanderer ever went that way
　　Except some cattle-ranger,
Or Indian of a former day,
Or settler discontent to stay,
　　Or (like myself) some stranger.

XIII.

Yet there, at rest, lay one who came,
　　Too weary for returning,—
Who bore, in death, that deathless name,
To which the Church's altar-flame
　　Is round the world kept burning.

XIV.

Who was the dead whose name alone
　　Thus stopped me as I wandered ?—
Whose life, unstoried on the stone,
Whose fortune, all untold, unknown,
　　I vaguely guessed and pondered.

XV.

The fate with which I grew beguiled
  Eluded my endeavor;
For was she babe?—or romping child?—
Or madcap maiden, free and wild,
  Now fallen asleep forever?

XVI.

Or was she one of wedded twain,
  Beloved and yet forsaken?—
Whom, lonely in the flowery-plain,
The westward toiling wagon-train
  Had left, since God had taken!

XVII.

Or was it age that bade her bow,
  Till,—old, and faint, and failing,—
She died a dame of wrinkled brow,
For whom th' unfurrowed prairie now
  Her furrowed face was veiling?
  5*

XVIII.

I only know that, short or long,

  Her life was with the humble,

Yet I enroll it with the throng

Of all who proudly live in song

  When brass and marble crumble.

XIX.

O Mary, like thy vernal clime,

  Whose year is un-Decembered,—

Forever blooming in its prime,—

So, never-withering be the rhyme

  That keeps thy name remembered!

XX.

—And what of him who, with his spade,

  Cleft open turf and gravel,

And dug the grave where she was laid,—

And heaped the hill, and knelt and prayed,—

  And joined his train of travel?

XXI.

Carved rudely on the slab of slate,
  The letters looked ungainly,—
Yet though the carver could not wait
To linger over day and date,
  He told his anguish plainly.

XXII.

O sorrow, keener than the knife
  That sculptured there its story!—
O woe that wept for child or wife!—
O mortal pain!—like human life,
  Ye too are transitory!

XXIII.

For God, in mercy to mankind,
  Endows the heart with feeling,
Yet lodges reason in the mind,
That man may have the wit to find
  For every hurt a healing.

XXIV.

The lightnings on the ocean play,
    And shoot their bolts of thunder,
And fleets are wrecked (the tidings say)—
Yet still the world goes on its way
    As if no ship went under.

XXV.

The chieftain falls,—and all his clan,
    Whom he had died defending,
Forget him for some lordlier man,— .
Whose glory, too, is but a span,
    And glimmers to an ending.

XXVI.

A little while, in grief forlorn,
    The empty-cradled mother
Sits mourning for her babe—new born—
Death-struck—and from her bosom torn,—
    Then smiles upon another.

XXVII.

The many-childed matron dies,
  Whose orphans kneel to kiss her,
And, while upon her bier she lies,
Anoint her with their weeping eyes,—
  Then cease to mourn or miss her.

XXVIII.

The bridegroom drops,—and, day and night,
  With sorrow unexceeded,
The bride bewails her widowed plight,—
Until, with heavy heart grown light,
  She is at last unweeded.

XXIX.

The heart, however great its grief,
  Or dearly this be cherished,
Or clung to for a season brief,
Soon sheds it like a loosened leaf
  That by the frost hath perished.

XXX.

The bleeding breast survives the blow,
　The pulses cease their raging,
The fever cools,—and so, we know,
There never comes a human woe
　But brings its own assuaging.

XXXI.

So what if Mary, in the mould,
　With carven stone above her,
Was wept when first her clay grew cold,
And mourned with sorrow manifold,
　By wedded lord or lover?—

XXXII.

Shall then a carping world upbraid,
　If he—though broken-hearted
When Mary in her grave was laid —
Thereafter, with another maid,
　Re-tied the cord that parted?

XXXIII.

There is a time for tears,—but then
　There comes a truce to sorrow:
It is the manly way of men,—
They love, and lose, and love again,
　And wed anew to-morrow.

XXXIV.

—I lay at rest an hour or more,
　But when the hounds, long hampered,
Began to whimper, and implore
To chase the bison as before,—
　I loosed them, and they scampered.

XXXV.

Hard after them, with leap and prance,
　I galloped down the prairie,—
And thought how strange a circumstance
That I, a stranger, was perchance .
　Sole mourner left for Mary!

THE JOY OF GRIEF.

THE JOY OF GRIEF.

I.

I HAD a grief too great for tears,
   And longed to weep, but tried in vain,
Until a monk, of snowy years,
   Appeared before me in my pain,
Who said, " Receive what I bestow,—
Heaven's balm for all who suffer so."

II.

Resenting madly, at the first,
   The blessing of the saintly sage,
" Depart from me—I am accurst ! "
   I answered, trembling in my rage ;

"Hath Heaven a balm?   I tell thee no!
Else why am I tormented so?"

III.

"My son," said he, "wring not thy hands,
　Beat not thy breast, tear not thy hair,
But lift to Heaven thy high demands,
　From knees as lowly as thy prayer,
And bounteous Heaven shall overflow
With showers of mercies on thee so."

IV.

"O monk, to Heaven my prayer I breathed,
　To grant me riches—honor—fame;
But straightway Heaven to me bequeathed
　A beggar's purse—a caitiff's name—
Ambition's fall—hope's overthrow—
And love's own wounds, now bleeding so!

V.

"Strip off, O monk, thy gown and hood!
　Fling down thy rosary to the dust!
There is no God—if God be good!
　There is no Heaven—if Heaven be just!
Life is but mockery here below—
If grief on grief can pierce it so!"

VI.

"Though life hath sorrow," quoth the friar,
　"Is death a boon for man to crave?
Then Heaven shall grant thy heart's desire,—
　For soon thy bones shall find a grave,
And from thy dust the grass shall grow,
And all thy pride be humbled so!"

VII.

Quoth I, "Since pain, with all its stings,
　Hath none to reach me underground,
Death, welcome as the peace he brings,
　Shall not, to me, come terror-crowned;

Nay, I to Death will shout, 'What ho!
What hath delayed thy coming so?'"

VIII.

Said he, "O sufferer, understand
   That thou art smitten of a rod
Not wielded by an angry hand,
   For He who scourgeth thee is God,—
Who loveth not to wound,—although
He needeth to chastise thee so."

IX.

I cried, "What is the need or gain
   Of all my anguish and despair?
What profit cometh of a pain
   That pierceth more than flesh can bear?
What can the tortured spirit owe
To tyrant Heaven that stings it so?"

X.

" My son," he whispered, " hear me speak :
  Doth God afflict but thee alone?
He heareth many a wilder shriek—
  He answereth many a deeper groan—
He striketh many a heavier blow—
He chasteneth thee and others so.

XI.

" For Life, like Death,—through all the world,
  In every age since Time began,—
With an unerring aim hath hurled
  A quivering dart at every man,
Till by the torture, swift or slow,
Mankind have all been tested so.

XII.

" Take solace of the saints of old ;—
  Of Daniel to the lions flung,—
Of Joseph into Egypt sold,
  Of Israel by the serpents stung ;—

If thou endure their trials,—lo!
Thou shalt partake their triumphs so!"

XIII.

Such lustre sparkled in his look
    That fear and reverence made me mute,
And courage so my heart forsook
    I ceased awhile from my dispute;
Then, forth like arrows from a bow,
I winged my questions thus and so:—

XIV.

"O monk, what is thy proffered balm
    But bitter mockery to my breast?—
For is an aching heart made calm,
    Or writhing spirit lulled to rest,
Because, in ages long ago,
The martyrs winced and quivered so?

XV.

" What if the fiery noonday sun
  Shall scorch the garden to a blight,
Until the fig-trees, one by one,
  All perish in the gardener's sight;—
Walks he among them, to and fro,
Consoled that Eden withered so?

XVI.

" What if the admiral's idle sail,
  That waits to catch the gentle breeze,
Be smitten of the bellowing gale
  Till whirlwinds whistle round the seas;—
Is it a solace, while they blow,
That ships of Tarshish foundered so?

XVII.

" What if the pilgrim's heavy pack
  Grow wearier with the lengthening road,
And galling to his aching back,
  Until he staggers with his load;—

Is he renewed in strength to know
That Gaza's gates were carried so?

XVIII.

" What if the stricken mother mourn
Because the darlings of her womb
Are from her ravished bosom torn
And cradled in th' unpitying tomb;—
Grieves she the less to lay them low
Since Rachel once outwept her so?

XIX.

" Though round the world, from east to west,
Each human heart, on shore or main,
My own among them, like the rest,
Should quiver to the self-same pain,—
How could the universal woe
Make *my* unhappy soul less so?

XX.

"Were I, at every grief I bear,
　To pray that Heaven would intervene
To give all other men a share,—
　I then would be as base and mean
As man's first murderer, long ago,—
Yea, far more fierce and cruel so!

XXI.

"Thrice worthier were the wish, in me,
　To suffer more, instead of less,
Could all the groaning world go free,
　Delivered through my one distress;—
Yea, I would Heaven itself forego,
To win it for my fellows so!"

XXII.

Said he, "O slow of heart, at last
　The balm thou seekest thou shalt find;

6

For if, with all the strength thou hast,

    Thou suffer nobly for mankind,

All pain which thou shalt undergo

Shall turn to bliss and rapture so!"

XXIII.

" Alas!" I murmured, "how can I,—

    So weak in wit, so poor in worth,

So little fit to live or die,—

    Win sweetly down from Heaven to earth

A blessing on a friend or foe

By virtue of my suffering so?'

XXIV.

With voice as sweet as when a song,

    Though ended, seems to echo still,

He whispered, "They who suffer long—

    And yet are patient—send a thrill

Through every soul to whom they show
The aureole of their sainthood so!

XXV.

" Then since no other balm avails
    To cool thy fever with a tear,
Remember thou the cross, the nails,
    The thorns, the vinegar, the spear,—
And sweet shall be thy bitterest throe
Because thy Master suffered so."

XXVI.

So tenderly he spoke the Name
    That all my tears began to start,
Till down my cheeks, that burned with shame,
    They rolled from my relenting heart
In drops as plenteous as the flow
Of Peter's who denied Him so.

XXVII.

Then down I fell, a guilty thing,
  Before an Angel in disguise,
Who, rustling each unfolding wing,
  Replumed it, radiant, for the skies,—
Upon whose pinions, white as snow,
I dared not look, they dazzled so!

PRINCE AND PEASANT.

PRINCE AND PEASANT.

I.

THE king of Bernicia, while hunting,
    Saw neither a fox, nor a boar,
But startled a fawn in the forest,
    That timidly ran before;
And this was the forester's daughter,
    Who fled to her father's door.

II.

The heart of her royal pursuer
    So throbbed with a rapturous beat
That, after the manner of lovers,
    In token of homage complete,

He knelt on the threshold before her,
  A prince at a peasant's feet.

III.

"O goddess," quoth he, "no mortal
  Can beauty like thine withstand!
For wilderness, river, and mountain
  Have moulded thee wild and grand!
So I, who am king of my kingdom,
  Sue here for thy heart and hand."

IV.

The virgin, all mute with marvel,
  Stood motionless like a tower!
And all through her cheeks ran changes,
  Like flushes that streak a flower!
And merely a moment of silence
  Seemed, all of a sudden, an hour!

V.

The forester spake for his daughter:
  "My liege, she is lowly born;
No dowry is hers for a portion,
  Nor jewels a bride to adorn;
Thou wooest to mock, not marry—
  Thou speakest in jest, or scorn."

VI.

Outwhipping his weapon in anger,
  The monarch replied with a frown,
"How darest thou brand me a jester,
  Or liken thy lord to a clown?
A king, when he wishes his wedding,
  May queen whom he will with his crown."

VII.

"O cease," said the maiden, "your quarrel!
  And bid me to love you both,—
6*

For why should a peasant's daughter
　　To marry a prince be loath?
O father, I plead for thy blessing—
　　O lover, I plight thee my troth."

VIII.

The king, though in Lincoln doublet,
　　As green as a summer elm,—
With neither his crest nor armor,—
　　With neither his crown nor helm,—
Yet looked as the Lord's anointed,
　　And ruler of all the realm.

IX.

" The boon of beauty to woman
　　Is given of Heaven," said he,
" But kings of the earth have bounty,
　　For they can give high degree;
Which I, as thy liege, O lady,
　　Give now unto thine and thee."

X.

He sent with a gleam to the scabbard
　　The blade he had drawn for a fight,
But not till he smote his foeman
　　To dub him a noble knight!—
(An honor that, save in romances,
　　Is seldom conferred on a wight.)

XI.

The monarch embraced the maiden,
　　Who tenderly clave and clung,—
Her hair, by the wind disheveled,
　　All hither and thither flung,—
And never were wilder lovers
　　Since time and the world were young!

XII.

" Prepare thee, O bride, for thy bridal,
　　Thou daughter," said he, " of an earl!

The earth, it shall give thee a diamond—
　The sea, it shall give thee a pearl—
And Heaven, it shall give thee a blessing,—
　O princess and peasant-girl !"

XIII.

The aisle of the old cathedral,
　That up to the altar led,
Was strewn for their feet with lilies,
　And thither they walked to be wed,—
In presence of throngs of the living,
　In presence of tombs of the dead.

XIV.

The bride-cake was big as a mountain,
　And virgins from near and far
Put crumbs of it under their pillows
　To dream of the lucky star
That dawns on a fortunate marriage,—
　Though marriages seldom are !

XV.

For since they are made in Heaven

(Or certes the proverb is wrong)

Of course they so very rarely

To earth, and to mortals, belong,

That perfectly married people

Wed only in story or song!

XVI.

Now as to the truth of the ditty,

If doubters be hard to convince,

Or deem it so very unlikely

A peasant could marry a prince,

Why, let them remember it happened

Some thousands of centuries since!

SHORTER POEMS.

THE LORD OF THE LAND.

THE gates of the city stood open wide,
And, just beyond, on the country side,
The beggars were huddled upon the grass,
Expecting the Lord of the Land to pass.
He often went out—he often came in,
But never with herald, nor trumpet's din:
He might be early—he might be late:
So always the beggars kept near the gate:
For so the poor on the rich must wait.

The crew was motley, and clad in rags:
The men were squalid—the women were hags;
The children were wasted to skin and bones;
The dogs had hungry and human tones!

On man and beast was poverty's blight !
Forlorn and pitiful was the sight !
And O, the mothers, with babes at the breast,
Looked far more wretched than all the rest !

The lord in his chariot rumbles by;
The beggars salute him with clamorous cry.
Will the horses halt?   Will the rider heed?
Will the rich befriend the poor in their need ?

The chariot stops, and the lord descends :
" I travel in haste," saith he, " my friends;
If you wait in hope of an alms to-day,
Speak quickly each, for I hurry away."

Cried one, " I am hungry—I ask for bread !"
The proud lord graciously answered and said :
" Poor soul, then go and knock at my door—
If hunger is all, thou shalt want no more."

Quoth a cripple, "My lord, I am lame, you see;
In charity, prithee remember *me*."
" Nay, charity cannot profit thee much—
I will help thee to do without thy crutch."

" My lord," cried one, " I am blind—I am blind;
So out of your bounty be kind, be kind !"
" Yea, help thee I can, and help thee I must;
Thine eyes shall be touched with a little dust,
And ever thereafter, O blinded man,
Thou shalt see as well as thy comrades can !"

Still closer about him pressed the crowd,—
With murmurs feeble, with clamors loud.

" I pray for a shelter, my lord,—I am old:
A corner to lie in, when nights are cold !"
" Old man, I have houses just out of the town—
Go choose thee a lodging, and lay thee down."

"My lord," said a lad, with thin, white palms,
"An orphan begs for a little alms!"
"My boy, thou art young, but ere thou art old,
I promise thee all thy hands can hold."

Quoth a stalwart man, "I am willing to toil;
So set me at work—I will dig your soil."
"A plot of my ground shall be thine in fee,
But another, O delver, shall dig it for thee."

A woman, too feeble to toil or spin,
Said, "Help me to go to my kith and kin!"
"Thy kith and kin I remember well—
I gladly will send thee to where they dwell."

"My lord," sighed a sufferer, sick and faint,
"I hardly have strength to utter complaint;
My fever is fiercer than I can bear—
I need physician, and nurse, and care."

"Go lie in my hospital on the hill,
And thou shalt be cured of every ill."

Thus flocked they around him, each urging a plea,
And never had beggars a bounty so free:
Whatever they asked for, he granted their prayer;
And even the dumb received their share,
Whose lips asked not, but whose piteous tale
Was told in their faces, haggard and pale.

Of all the rabble, the last who spoke
Was the nakedest carl of the ragged folk:
"My lord," he clamored, "I beg for a cloak!"

The great lord answered, with pitying tone,
"I cannot deny thee—take my own!"
Then, doffing his mantle of sable-black,
He flung it over the beggar's back!

The uncloaked lord, by this wild whim,

Stood forth a skeleton, gaunt and grim!

The beggars, astounded, gasped for breath,

And knew that their bountiful friend was Death.

THE WANDERER'S SONG.

I.

THROUGH many a kingdom and city and land,
I travel away from the clasp of thy hand ;
But whether on mountain or river or sea,—
Wherever I wander, my heart is with thee !

II.

The purple and gold at the break of the day,
The sparkle of dew-drops that sprinkle my way,
The bloom on the meadow, the bud on the tree,—
Whatever hath beauty reminds me of thee !
143

III.

The trill of the lark as he soars to the sky,
The sigh of the pine as the wind fleeth by,
The hymn of the locust, the hum of the bee,—
Whatever makes melody whispers of thee!

IV.

If I, as a bard, strike a note of my own,
Of banquet and laughter, of battle and groan,
My song is a love-song, whatever the key,—
Whatever I sing of, I sing it for thee!

V.

The brow of the mower is beaded with sweat,—
His task is a hardship, his toil is a fret;
But light as a feather my load is to *me*,—
Whatever the burden, I bear it for thee!

VI.

The air is enchanted wherever I go—
Thyself the enchantress who charmeth it so!—
And bountiful Nature is buoyant and free
Because her own spirit is borrowed of thee!

VII.

Without thee the world would be empty and drear,
For thou art the blessing that gives it its cheer!
I care not what fortune the Fates may decree,—
My treasure of treasures is only in thee!

VIII.

Of all the fair fancies that flit through my brain,
That come and go quickly, too bright to remain,
One vanisheth never, though others may flee,—
And this is the image, my darling, of thee!

7

IX.

To love thee in absence is rapture of bliss :

Then what were thy presence, and what were thy

     kiss?

—From mountain to river, from river to sea,

I hasten, my darling, I hasten to thee!

LYRA INCANTATA.

I.

WITHIN a castle haunted
(As castles were of old)
There hung a harp enchanted,
And, on its rim of gold,
This legend was enscrolled:
"Whatever bard would win me,
Must strike and wake within me,
By one supreme endeavor,
A chord that sounds forever."

II.

Three bards of lyre and viol,
By mandate of the king,

Were bidden to a trial
　　To find the magic string—
　　(If there were such a thing).
　　　Then, after much essaying
　　　Of tuning, came the playing;
　　　And lords and ladies splendid
　　　Watched as those bards contended.

III.

The first, a minstrel hoary—
　　Who many a rhyme had spun—
Sang loud of war and glory,
　　Of battles fought and won:
　　But when his song was done,
　　　Although the bard was lauded,
　　　And clapping hands applauded,
　　　Yet, spite of the laudation,
　　　The harp ceased its vibration.

IV.

The second changed the measure,
　And turned from fire and sword
To sing a song of pleasure,—
　　The wine-cup and the board:
　　Till, at his wit, all roared,
　　　And the high hall resounded
　　　With merriment unbounded!
　　　The harp, loud as the laughter,
　　　Grew hushed as that, soon after!

V.

The third,—in lover's fashion,
　And with his soul on fire,—
Then sang of love's pure passion,—
　　The heart and its desire:
　　And, as he smote the wire,

The listeners, gathering round him,
Caught up a wreath and crowned him!
The crown—hath faded never!
The harp—resounds forever!

AMONG THE REEDS.

I.

Swim fast, O wounded swan, swim fast!
Thy mate awaits thee in her nest,—
·Not dreaming that the dart was cast
Which quivers in thy bleeding breast!

II.

Swim fast, O dying swan, swim fast!
Die not till she beholds thy fate,—
Lest she may deem some fickle blast
Hath blown thee to another mate!

III.

Swim fast, O faithful swan, swim fast!
  The adverse tide is swift and strong!
Swim fast, swim fast, until at last
  Thou sing to her thy dying song!

LONESOME.

I.

I WANDER by the sparkling stream
That shimmers in the morning sun,
But all the glitter and the gleam
Now mock me like an empty dream,—
Through thinking of an absent one.

II.

I listen to the robin's note,
But find no music in his lay,
For though he hath a merry throat,
And many lovers on him dote,
Yet *my* true lover is away.

III.

I pluck the sweet and dewy rose,
  But, spite of all the dews of morn,
No sweetness in a bud that blows
Remaineth when my lover goes,—
  Whose going leaves my heart forlorn.

IV.

I weary of the clouds that fly,
  I weary of the winds that roar,
I weary of the earth and sky,
I weary of my own sad sigh,—
  Till my true lover comes once more!

FLOWN.

O Dove of Peace, thou long ago
    Wert wont, on many a weary day,
To brood so sweetly on my woe
    That half the pain was charmed away!
Then rudely did I thee affright,
    And roughly did I thee affray,—
Till thou wert driven to seek, by flight,
    Some gentler friend with whom to stay.
But now I bend my straining sight,
    As twilight falls on bank and brae,
To watch until thy pinions white
    Gleam toward me through the evening gray!
Fly downward from thy heavenly height,
    To be again my holy guest!

Where wilt thou on the earth alight,
    If not in a repentant breast?
Haste hither to a heart contrite
    To lull its restlessness to rest!
Come fold thy wings with me to-night,
    And let my bosom be thy nest!

CROSS AND CRESCENT.

I.

"Down with the Infidel abhorred!
Up with the banner of the Lord!"
 So the Crusaders sang,
As into Palestine they poured,—
 While, with defiant clash and clang,
 Their swords and bucklers rang.

II.

"Death to the Christian dogs!" replied
The scornful Moslems, in their pride;

"Let Allah's host advance!"
Then, in the sunshine,—far and wide,—
Like summer lightning was the glance
Of scimetar and lance.

III.

Fair Heaven on both their armies smiled,
And wished the foemen reconciled;
But, in their pious rage,
Each by the other was reviled,—
Till now, in wrath, from age to age,
Eternal war they wage.

IV.

How can the sacred discord end?
How can the Cross and Crescent blend?
How can the trumpet cease
That calls their pennons to contend?
O Crescent, wane! O Cross, increase!
From Truth alone comes Peace!

V.

The whole Creation groans with pain
Till He whose right it is shall reign!
When shall His reign begin?
When shall the chariots quit the plain?
O Cross, above the battle's din,
Thy peaceful triumph win!

VI.

A little child, with shepherd's crook,
Through pastures green, by water-brook,
Shall Lamb and Lion lead:
So saith thy promise, Holy Book!
Then, since the word is fair to read,
Fulfill it with the deed!

THE BARD'S LISTENER.

I.

I STRUNG my lyre
With golden wire,
To sing a song of pure desire:
A maiden heard
Whose soul was stirred
Until her bosom glowed with fire.

II.

" How can it be
That chant and glee
Have such a dangerous power?" quoth she.
160

—My lyre, that day,

She stole away,

And hid it under lock and key.

III.

" Why do you hide

My harp?" I cried.

—" Because," the blushing maid replied,

" I seek to know

Which thrilled me so,

The song or singer ? "—and she sighed.

IV.

The long day fled,

And back I sped

To ask, at eve, with hope and dread,—

" Which was it ? pray !

The bard or lay ? "

—" I quite forgot you both ! " she said.

MARGERY'S BEADS.

I.

Quoth I to pretty Margery More,
" Where are the beads that once you wore ? "

II.

Gay Margery sighed, and drooped her head,
And with a mournful murmur said:

III.

" I counted lovers,—one, two, three,—
Each swearing he would die for me.

IV.

" I then devised a cruel test

To prove which lover loved me best :

V.

" I held my beads above a well,

And let them slip, and down they fell.

VI.

"' Leap in ! ' cried I, ' my pretty men,

And bring me up my beads again ! '

VII.

" I tried to guess which youth would dive,

And come up, panting, half alive !

VIII.

" But love makes every man a fool :

All three dove down into the pool !

IX.

"The pool was deep,—they all were drowned,—
And never were their bodies found !

X.

"What maid was ever punished so?"
And Margery's tears began to flow.

XI.

Long, long the maid, whom Fate had robbed
Of her three lovers, sat and sobbed.

XII.

"Sad heart," quoth I, "grieve not so sore—
You.yet may find three lovers more."

XIII.

"Alas!" quoth she, "my bosom bleeds,
Not for my lovers, but my beads!"

THE FOUR SEASONS.

I.

In the balmy April weather,

    My love, you know,

    When the corn began to grow,

What walks we took together,

What sighs we breathed together,

What vows we pledged together,

    In the days of long ago!

II.

In the golden summer weather,

    My love, you know,

    When the mowers went to mow,

What home we built together,

What babes we watched together,

What plans we planned together,

　While the skies were all aglow!

III.

In the rainy autumn weather,

　My love, you know,

　When the winds began to blow,

What tears we shed together,

What mounds we heaped together,

What hopes we lost together,

　When we laid our darlings low!

IV.

In the wild and wintry weather,

　My love, you know,

　With our heads as white as snow,

What prayers we pray together,

What fears we share together,

What Heaven we seek together,

    For our time has come to go!

THE ARTLESS ART.

I.

I SANG my lady many a lay
  To win her by the music in it,
But word and tune were thrown away,
Till, haply on a morn in May,
  I chanced to hear a singing linnet.

II.

Now many a bird of brighter coat
  May plume himself on his apparel,
But never in a warbler's throat
Was trilled a more enchanting note
  Than quivered in that linnet's carol.

III.

" O tiny, passion-tortured thing,

   Thy song," quoth I, "hath all its rapture

Because thou amorously dost sing—

In these, the wooing days of spring—

   Thy velvet-mantled mate to capture.

IV.

" With song like thine, O bonny bird,

   If I could sing it half so sweetly,

Then, haply, if my lady heard,

Her stony bosom would be stirred,

   And I would win her love completely.

V.

" So I implore thee to impart

   Unto thy ruder brother-poet

The secret of the songful art

To charm a lady's haughty heart

   Till on the singer she bestow it."

8

VI.

" No art is mine to tell thee of,"
　The songster said, " for I disdain it :
Go ask the robin—ask the dove—
Ask every bird that sings of love :
　We feel it, but we never feign it.

VII.

" Then go and woo as song-birds do,
　Who, from the seed-time to the sickle,
Love faithfully the season through,
Nor change the *old* love for a new,
　Nor prove (as men do) false and fickle.

VIII.

" Forbear a poet's fatal pride
　In praising every charmer's beauty,
But ever to thy chosen bride,—
To her alone, and none beside,—
　Sing thou a song of love and duty."

IX.

On that same day, with hope elate,
  Beneath an arbor green and shady,
To that same maid who held my fate,—
Like that same linnet to his mate,
  I sang my lay, and won my lady!

IN GOD'S ACRE.

I.

THOU art alive, O grave,—
Thou with thy living grass,
Blown of all winds that pass,—
Thou with thy daisies white,
Dewy at morn and night,—
Thou on whose granite stone
Greenly the moss has grown,—
Thou on whose holy mound,
Through the whole summer round,
Sweetly the roses thrive,—
Thou art alive !
O grave, thou art alive !

172

II.

Answer me, then, O grave,—

Yea, from thy living bloom

Speak to me, O green tomb,—

Say if the maid I know,

Sepulchred here below,—

Say if the sweet white face,

Hidden in this dark place,—

Say if the hair of gold

Buried amid thy mould,—

Say, O thou grave, her bed,—

Is my love dead ?

O say, are the dead dead?

FLUTE AND LUTE.

A LOVER, with flute,
And a lady, with lute,
    Sat playing in discord together;
And the wind rose high
In the cloudy sky,
    And winterish was the weather!

        " If it be love (sang she)
        If it be love,
            Tell me, Is thine
            Equal to mine?
            Give me some sign
        If it be love."
                    174

" If it be love (piped he)
If it be love,
    Keep it at rest
    Deep in thy breast,
    Asking no test
If it be love."

Then, sweeter than lute,
And softer than flute,
    Their lips came close together;
And the clouds rolled by,
And blue was the sky,
    And sunshiny was the weather!

BONAVENTURA.

I.

" COME tell me my fortune!—and when it is told,

Though *some* give you silver, yet *I* will give gold :

My lover afar—is he faithful ? O say !—

Then why doth he loiter so long on the way?"

II.

" I see, by thy hand, that thy lover shall ride

From over the desert to make thee his bride !

Like dew to the bud, or the bud to the bee,

So thou to thy lover, thy lover to thee !"

III.

The teller of fortunes flung off his disguise,

And *there* stood her lover, with love in his eyes!

Then each of their fortunes, more precious than
    gold,

Was just what the arms of two lovers could hold!

8*

CUPID'S PUZZLE.

I.

A MAID, who was milking her cow in the clover,

Kept warbling a love-ditty over and over,—

And this was the song that she sang:

" O would there were love, without plague of a

lover!

For love, without lover, if *so* it could be,

Were love without trouble and torment," quoth

she,

" And this is the love for *me!* "

Then, patting her cow,

She uttered a vow,—

" I never will marry, but tarry as now!

My heart is my own, and my fancy is free;
And as for a sailor forever at sea,
What kind of a lover is *he?* "

II.

Then, softly behind her, there stole through the
    clover
A sailor, just landed from all the seas over,
Who forward in front of her sprang:
" My darling, behold me, thy truant true lover!
And here is the ring that I promised to thee!—
And when, at the church, thou art wedded to *me*,
Farewell to the rolling sea!"
Now maids are inclined
To changes of mind;
So she, who was cruel, turned suddenly kind!
" His heart is as faithful as ever," thought she.
"·Her cheek is as red as a cherry," thought he,
" Or bud of a blush-rose tree!"

III.

Then after the wedding had come, and was over,

She frequently patted her cow in the clover,

And this was the song that she sang:

" Now what do I love?—is it love, or my lover?—

Which *is* it, I wonder, or *ought* it to be?

It puzzles me, *that* or *he ?* "

The question grew deep as the sea,—

For never the bride

Knew how to divide

The love in her heart from the man at her side.

" What is it a woman loves best ? " quoth she:

" Herself, and her love, and her lover—all three!

And this is the love for *me !* "

"A FRIEND IN NEED IS A FRIEND INDEED."

I.

THE old Taff tavern had for a sign,
A faded flagon of painted wine,
With a mouldy motto that meant to read,—
"A friend in need is a friend indeed."

II.

When farmer, fisher, and hunter were there,
To mingle their mirth, or kill their care,—
However they wrangled, in this they agreed:
"A friend in need is a friend indeed."

III.

They drank to the tavern-sign, one day,—
Till mugs of pewter and pipes of clay
Made foam of liquor and fume of weed:
"A friend in need is a friend indeed."

IV.

"Then here's to the truest of friends!" said one:
"What friend hath a hunter so true as his gun?
It renders him service with uttermost speed:
'A friend in need is a friend indeed.'"

V.

"But what if thy powder, my lad, be wet?
No fair-weather friend is a fisherman's net!
Mine earneth me many a tankard of mead:
'A friend in need is a friend indeed.'"

VI.

" Thy gun is a slayer—thy net is a snare:
Of friends so bloody and crafty, beware!
The plough!—It toileth the hungry to feed:
'A friend in need is a friend indeed.'"

VII.

Then, thumping the table, they said with a laugh,
" Now who shall decide it but Grandfather Taff?—
For *he* is the landlord who lives by the creed,
'A friend in need is a friend indeed.'"

VIII.

" Say, which is a man's best friend?" they cried,
" The gun, or the net, or the plough?—Decide!—
The young should unto the old give heed:
'A friend in need is a friend indeed.'"

IX.

" What fools," cried the patriarch, "young men
  are !
I drink to the buxom maid of the bar,
Whom I to the altar to-morrow shall lead !
' A friend in need is a friend indeed.' "

RECOMPENSE.

THE Temple of the Lord stood open wide,
And worshippers went up from many lands,
Who, kneeling at the altar, side by side,
Made votive offerings with uplifted hands.

Their gifts were gold, and frankincense, and myrrh.

Then, with a lustrous gleam and rapturous stir,
While all the people trembled and turned pale,
There flew an Angel to the altar-rail,
Who, with anointed eyes, keen to discern,

Gazed, noting all the kneelers, who they were,
And what was each one's tribute to the Lord,—
And, gift for gift, with sudden, swift return,
Bestowed on every suppliant his reward.

O mocking recompense! To one, a spear!
To many, each a thorn! To some, a nail!
To all, a cross! But unto none, a crown!

At last, they saw the Angel disappear.

Then, as their timid hearts shook off their fear,
Some rose in anger, flung their treasures down,
And cried, "Such gifts from Heaven as these, we
      spurn!
They are too cruel, and too keen to bear!
They are too grievous for a human breast!
Heaven sends us heartache, misery, and despair!
We knelt for blessing, but we rise unblest!
If Heaven so mock us, we will cease to pray!"

They left the altar, and they went their way;
But their blaspheming hearts were then self-torn
Far more by pride, and heaven-defying scorn,
Than pierced before by nail, or spear, or thorn!

A few (not many!) with their brows down bent,
Gave thanks for each sharp gift that Heaven had
      sent,—
And each embraced his separate pain and sting,
As if it were some sweet and pleasant thing,—
And each his cross, with joyful tears, did take,
To bear it for the great Cross-bearer's sake.

Then lo! as from the Temple forth they went,
Their bleeding bosoms, though with anguish rent,
Had, spite of all their pain!—a sweet content;
For on each brow, though not to mortal sight,
The vanished Angel left a crown of light!

THE THREE FATES.

Clotho.........*Birth.*
Lachesis.... ...*Life.*
Atropos ....*Death.*

I.

Let me sing a sullen hymn
To the Triple Sisters grim!
Never since the world began,
Were they gentle unto man!
Never till the world shall end,
Will they be a mortal's friend!
Since they oft have done me wrong,
I will chide them with a song!

188

II.

Clotho,—oldest of the old,
Wierd and hateful to behold,—
Doth a distaff ever twirl,
Whence is spun, at every whirl,
Subtile yarn, so fine and white
That it baffles human sight,—
Yet it twineth round, at birth,
Every babe born on the earth!—
For, when Clotho sits and spins,
Then the thread of life begins.

III.

Close beside her,—fierce of mien,
Wild and haggard, wan and lean,—
Lachesis, her sister, stands—
With her spindle in her hands:

Measuring out to every man,
Brief or long, his mortal span!—
Reeling forth from off the coil
Just his term of life and toil!

IV.

Atropos,—whose ghastly face
Frighteneth all the human race,—
Waiteth till the hour draws nigh
When a mortal man must die:
Then, all heedless of his tears,
Hastening thither with her shears,
Ruthlessly she cuts the thread,—
And her victim droppeth dead!

V.

O ye spectral Sisters Three,
What remains unwound for *me?*—
Clotho hath her portion spun!—
Lachesis will soon be done!—

Atropos is near, and waits!

—Yet as what ye spin, O Fates,

Is but poor and worthless stuff,—

Now my thread is long enough!

THE MYSTIC MESSAGE.

A WILD-EYED virgin, strange in her attire,
Watched the crusading hosts, in their advance,
And gazed from line to line, from lance to lance,
With eager look to see the king of France;
Whom, when she spied, she knelt to, saying, " Sire,
I bring to thee, through forest, moor, and mire,
This vase of water, and this torch of fire!"

The wondering king upraised her from her knees,
Received her gifts, and asked, " Why bring you
these?"

" My liege," she answered, " at the dead of night,
There came an angel, clad in shining white,

Who called to me and said, ' O child of grace,

The Lord Christ grieveth for the human race,—

For He appeals to mortal men in vain

Except through hope of bliss, or fear of bane :

Why seek they Heaven ? For love of God ? Not so ;

But only for the bliss they hope to gain !

Why shun they Hell ? For hate of evil ? No ;

But only to escape the woe and pain !

Wherefore, O child, at the Lord Christ's desire,

Arise ! He hath for thee an errand ! Go !—

Go with swift feet that loiter not, nor tire,—

Go as the wild hare runs through brake and brier,—

Go as the swallow speeds upon the wing,—

Go bear two emblems to the pious king :

One, this fierce flambeau that shall hotly burn,

And one, this cool, full, brimming water-urn :

Give both into the king's own mighty hand :

Then bid him whirl, three times, the burning brand—

Round, round, and round his head—and let it fly

Straight at the very zenith of the sky,

9

To set high heaven on fire, and burn it low,
Till all its crumbled walls with ashes glow,
And not a gate remain to enter by!
Then bid him from the brimming urn outpour
The water through some crevice in earth's floor,
Down, down, deep down into the depths of hell,
Whose fire these cooling drops shall quench and
    quell,
That those eternal flames may blaze no more!'

"This do, O king, at the Lord Christ's behest,
Till round the rolling earth, from east to west,
Shall neither Heaven nor Hell by man be known,
But God be worshipped for Himself alone!"

Her errand done,—with sudden leap and bound
The virgin vanished out of sight and sound!

This tale in olden chronicles is found ;

And if the maid was daft (as there is writ)

Much wisdom often lies in little wit.

SIR MARMADUKE'S MUSINGS.

I.

I WON a noble fame;

But, with a sudden frown,

The people snatched my crown,

And, in the mire, trod down

My lofty name.

II.

I bore a bounteous purse;

And beggars by the way ·

Then blessed me, day by day;

But I, grown poor as they,

Have now their curse.

196

III.

I gained what men call friends;
    But now their love is hate,
    And I have learned, too late,
    How mated minds unmate,
And friendship ends.

IV.

I clasped a woman's breast,—
    As if her heart, I knew,
    Or fancied, would be true,—
    Who proved, alas! she too!
False like the rest.

V.

I now am all bereft,—
    As when some tower doth fall,
    With battlement, and wall,
    And gate, and bridge, and all,—
And nothing left.

VI.

But I account it worth
    All pangs of fair hopes crossed—
    All loves and honors lost,—
    To gain the heavens, at cost
Of losing earth.

VII.

So, lest I be inclined
    To render ill for ill,—
    Henceforth in me instil,
    O God, a sweet good will
To all mankind.

SHIPWRECK.

A LOVER'S bosom is a billowy deep,
Whereon the breath of doubt, the gust of pride,
The storm of tears so often rudely sweep
That halcyon peace doth seldom there abide;
For suddenly the purple sails, spread wide,
Of shallops laden with the heart's whole gain,
Are struck of tempest in the middle main,
And silver masts are split, and silken ropes
Are sundered,—yea, and many an anchor chain,
Deemed adamant, is snapped,—until, at last,
Down fathomless go freights of foundering hopes,
All sunk in dismal caverns, deep and vast,—
Whence, ever upward to a barren shore,
Sad tides cast wrecks of memories,—nothing more!

SERENADE.

I.

Open thy casement, and list to my lute!
    Its music, O lady, is vain—
    And better by far were mute—
    Unless thou wilt hear the strain.

II.

Peep through thy lattice, and show me thy face!
    For shortly the setting moon
    Will shadow thy beauty's grace—
    So, show it, fair lady, soon!

200

III.

Down from thy balcony fling me a rope!
    I linger, I long, I wait,
    With love and a lover's hope,
    For love and a lover's fate.

9*

THE TWO ROADS.

IT was the parting of the ways:
I chose the left—a flowery maze,
When, all at once, before my sight,
A stranger pointed to the right.

Was it a warning that he meant?
I heeded not, but on I went,
And journeyed gayly, half the morn,
Until I trod upon a thorn.

Its dagger pierced me to the quick,
And drops of blood came fast and thick:
I dried them with a balsam-flower,
And sat and suffered for an hour.

Then up I leaped, and onward strode,
Still keeping to the self-same road,—
Through roses blowing or full-blown,—
And dashed my foot against a stone.

I slipped, I fainted, and I fell,—
And lay—how long I cannot tell—
Till, waking with bewildered look,
I spied a purling wayside brook,
Wherein I bathed my throbbing sore,—
And started on my way once more.
Then, through a shady sylvan scene,
Turfed softly with a tender green,
I strayed awhile—until, alas!
A serpent stung me in the grass!

With sudden horror, pain, and dread
I turned me from the spot and fled,
And all my wayward steps retraced
Until I reached, with panting haste,

The primal parting of the ways;

Where, once again, to my amaze,

I saw the self-same stranger stand,

Still pointing with his steadfast hand;

Who said, " How woeful is the plight

Of feet that stray, though guided right!

If on this road thou travel more,

Note all the pointings—they are four:

The first, my hand—so plain to see

That if to this thou givest heed,

The other three thou shalt not need:

If this be spurned,—the other three,—

Thorn, flint, and sting!—shall point for thee!"

EXPIATION.

Fair lady, if the asp on Egypt's breast,

That stung the sad queen to her welcome death,—

If that unheeding worm had only guessed

Whose heart it was he gnawed with such a zest,—

What royal bosom yielded him its breath,—

He would have stung his venomed self instead,

As other serpents do : and so will I !

For since, O queenlier queen, since thou hast said

That I have wound my serpentining way

To thy imperial heart, to sting and slay,—

I make to thy reproaches this reply :

Not thou, my queen, but I, thy worm, shall die !

I spare the bosom where I lay my head !

Farewell ! Live thou !—for I, self-stung, am dead !

THE TRYSTING-PLACE.

I.

WHILE they lingered, he and she,
Underneath their linden tree,—
Twilight fell on land and sea.

II.

Trembling, as the color fled
Swiftly from her lips of red,—
" Kiss me not again !" she said.

III.

He, unheedful of her prayer,
Kissed her madly, then and there,—
Lips, and cheeks, and brow, and hair !

IV.

" Let me go," cried she, " I pray—
It is late—I dare not stay!"
With a leap she sprang away!

V.

With a swifter leap sprang he—
Caught her—clasped her—bent his knee—
Vowed his vow—and plead his plea!

VI.

Did she frown and answer nay?
Did she smile and whisper yea?
Not a word had she to say!

VII.

But a maid who sinks to rest
Mutely on her lover's breast
Leaves her answer to be guessed.

VIII.

Never fell the evening dew,
Since in Eden love was new,
On a love more pure and true.

IX.

When those lovers, hand in hand,
Went from where those lindens stand,
Morning dawned on sea and land.

THE FRENCH LESSON.

I.

SHALL I teach you French, my dear?
Sit and con your lesson here:
What did Adam say to Eve?
Aimer, aimer, ah! c'est vivre!

II.

Don't roll out the last word long—
Make it short to suit the song—
Rhyme it to your flowing sleeve!—
Aimer, aimer, ah! c'est vivre!

III.

Sleeve is used in France for arm—
Arm, for waist—so would it harm
Just to clasp you?—by your leave?—
Aimer, aimer, ah! c'est vivre!

IV.

Speaking French is full of slips—
Do as *I* do with the lips:
Here's the method, you perceive!—
Aimer, aimer, ah! c'est vivre!

V.

Pretty pupil, when you say
All this French to me to-day,
Do you mean it, or deceive?—
Aimer, aimer, ah! c'est vivre!

VI.

Aimer, that's to love, you know!
Say it to me soft and low!
Make me feel that you believe
Aimer, aimer, ah! c'est vivre!

VII.

For in France, you understand,
When they press each other's hand,
Then their hearts together cleave!—
Aimer, aimer, ah! c'est vivre!

VIII.

Bride of beauty, in your hair
You shall orange-blossoms wear!
When shall I the garland weave?
Aimer, aimer, ah! c'est vivre!

IX.

Sweetheart, do not rise to go—
Sit and let me hold you so!
Adam did the same to Eve!—
Aimer, aimer, ah! c'est vivre!

THE GOATHERD'S GIFT.

To thee, fair Shepherdess, I bring this rose,—

This red and fiery flower of love, that grows

For all true lovers, and is love's own sign

Whereby whoever gives or takes it knows

 That both their hearts are one,—like mine and

  thine.

I say, like mine and thine: Do I presume?

 Or am I over-bold? O maiden mine,—

If mine thou art, then wear my rose,—whose

  bloom,

(That borrows thine), is love's own type!—Behold!

Though rains, and storms, and tempests manifold

With all their floods this burning flower have
    drenched,
Yet all their many waters have not quenched
    Its ever-quenchless fire,—like love's own flame!
    So take my rose,—and find my love the same!

THE FORLORN HOPE.

I.

OUT of twenty in the fray,

That morn,—

To their burial ten, that night,

Were borne ;

And their faces, toward the moon,

Looked pale,—

And the night-wind murmured forth

Its wail !

" We are beaten—we are flying—

We are wounded—we are dying—

Yet we cannot leave them lying

With no word of blessing said ! "

215

So, the soldiers all complying,
    Then the Sergeant bared his head,
    And he read the holy service
    For the burial of the dead.

II.

" Is there any other prayer
    To pray?
Is there any other word
    To say?
Is there any other sod
    To bring?
Is there any other flower
    To fling?
  " We must do it now, or never!
  For at midnight we must sever—
  We must scatter—and endeavor
    Each to flee a separate way!

Since the dead are safe forever,
  Save yourselves, if so ye may!"
  And they left their buried comrades,
  And escaped ere break of day.

10

THE DEAD POET.*

Is this the only tribute we should pay?—

   These funeral flowers that on his bier belong?

   Himself a singer, he deserves a song;

But who has any heart to sing to-day?

Should any stranger chance to come this way,

   And view with tearless eyes this lump of earth,

 . And call for witness to its living worth,

Our grief would choke the words that we would

     say!

   Let us be silent—like our silent dead;

Whose virtues,—Truth, Faith, Honor, and the

     rest,—

---

* The above lines were written on the occasion of the funeral of
William Henry Burleigh.

With one loud-chanted requiem, all have said :

" Behold, our chosen dwelling was his breast!"

Since tongues like these have spoken, dumb be

ours :

So let us sweetly leave him with his flowers.

THE TWO LADDERS.

BENIGHTED in my pilgrimage,—alone,—
  And footsore—(for the path to Heaven grew
    steep,)—
I looked for Jacob's pillow of a stone,
  In hope of Jacob's vision in my sleep.
Then, in my dream, whereof I quake to tell,—
  Not up from earth to Heaven, but, O sad
    sight!
The ladder was let down from earth to hell!—
  Whereon, ascending from the deep abyss,
  Came fiery spirits who, with dismal hiss,
Made woeful clamor of their lost delight,
And stung my eyelids open, till, in fright,

I caught my staff, and at the dead of night,

    I, who toward Heaven and peace had halted so,

    Was fleet of foot to flee from Hell and woe!

ASTRAY.

I TRAVELED a forbidden road,
Which first appeared so flowery fair
That onward eagerly I strode
Till,—to my horror and despair !—
All buds and blossoms, blooming there,
All tender boughs and twigs of green
Stood changed to burrs and nettles keen,—
Whose angry points my garments tore,
And pricked my hands till they were sore.

Bewildered at the wondrous change,
That should have warned me from the place,
I kept my course with swifter pace,
And saw a marvel still more strange ;

For cruel flints sprang through the ground

To meet my feet at every bound,

With gash on gash that made them bleed.

Then time it was that I should heed!

Just at the moment of my need,

A shining man stood at my side,—

Whose lustre fell on all around,

And spread a glory far and wide!

" And who art thou?" I trembling cried.

" Give ear," said he, " to what I say:

I am the guide of all who stray,

To point them back to virtue's path,—

The guardian of thy erring way;

And, step by step,—in love, not wrath,—

These angry flints and briers I strew,

To warn thy feet from wandering so."

I knelt and kissed his garment's hem,
And cried, "O angel, sent from Heaven!
Make sharper yet each thorny stem!
Increase the flints to seven times seven!—
Fulfil thy purpose in my pain—
I will endure, and not complain!"

He fled!—and I, with deep remorse,
Turned back from my forbidden course,—
But, O how many weary hours
I traveled ere those blighted bowers
Re-bloomed with all their former flowers!

THE KING'S COURAGE.

I.

King Dionysius reigned in Syracuse,
    As ancient chroniclers have curtly told,
Who mention also that his life was loose,
    Till his transgressions grew so manifold
    That Plato, the philosopher, made bold
To tell him, at the risk of being rude,
That kings, through luxury, lose fortitude!
    But the philosopher, though wise, was wrong:
    The royal reveler did a deed, ere long,
    The bravest ever sung by poet's song.

II.

For where there is a will, there is a way;
  At least, if that old proverb tells the truth:
So Dionysius fixed his wedding-day,
  And cried, " A lack of fortitude, forsooth !
  Does Plato take me for a limpid youth?
O great philosopher, thou art a dunce!"
The King—who loved two women—both at once—
  Stood up between them—one on either side—
  And marrying both, endured each jealous bride,
  And lived, a hero, after Plato died!

FABELLA.

THE high heavens listened to the earth
To hear its sounds and note their worth.
A lark trilled forth his roundelay
Just as an ass began to bray.
Each hushed his own astonished throat,
Bewildered at the other's note.
The scornful bird said to the brute,
" Thou pipest on a wheezy flute."
The brute replied, " Thou hast, O bird,
The sweetest note I ever heard."
This colloquy reached to the ears
Of all the listening upper spheres.
When next the lark sang in the sky,
He heard a voice say from on high :
227

" Think not thy haughty notes surpass
The modest matins of the ass :
The high heavens love a lowly mind,—
In bird, in beast, in human kind."

TRANSLATIONS.

SIR OLAF.

FROM THE GERMAN OF HEINE.

(Translated in the original metres.)

I.

AT the door of the cathedral
Stand two men together, waiting;
Both are clad in scarlet raiment;
One the king, and one the headsman.

And the king saith to the headsman,
"From the psalm the priests are singing,
Now methinks the marriage ended;
—Headsman, hold thy good axe ready!"

Clang of bells, and peal of organ!
Forth the folk stream from the temple:
Motley is the throng,—and, midway,
Come the bridal-pair, bejeweled.

Pale, and full of fear and sorrow
Looks the king's all-beauteous daughter;
Bluff and blithesome looks Sir Olaf,—
And his red mouth, it is smiling!

And with smiling red mouth, saith he
To the king, who standeth scowling,
"Sire, thy son bids thee good morning!
Thou, this day, my head requirest:

"I, this day, must die! O let me
Live the day through till the midnight,
That my nuptials I may honor
With a wedding-feast and torch-dance!

" Let me, let me live, I pray thee,

Till the last cup shall be emptied—

Till the last dance shall be finished!—

Let me live until the midnight!"

And the king saith to the headsman,

" To our son we grant a respite—

Let him live until the midnight!

—Headsman, hold thy good axe ready!"

II.

Sir Olaf at the festive board

Drains the last flagon that is poured;

Close clingeth to his side

His sobbing bride!

—Before the door stands the headsman!

The waltz begins; and Sir Olaf the waist

Of his young wife clasps, and away—in wild

haste—

They whirl to the glitter and glance
Of the last torch-dance!
—Before the door stands the headsman!

The blare of the trumpets is loud and glad;
The sigh of the flutes is soft and sad;
Each guest, beholding the dancing twain,
Feels a shiver of pain.
—Before the door stands the headsman!

And while they dance in the echoing room,
To the ear of the bride thus whispers the groom,
" How dearly I love thee can never be told—
The grave is so cold!"
—Before the door stands the headsman!

III.

Sir Olaf, it is noon of night!
Thy life has filled its measure:
Thou with the daughter of a prince
Hast had unhallowed pleasure!

The monks, with murmuring voice, begin
The·prayer for the dead's redeeming;
The man in red, on a scaffold black,
Stands with his white axe gleaming.

Sir Olaf strides to the castle-yard :
The lights and the swords shine brightly;
The red mouth of the knight, it smiles !—
And he crieth gayly and lightly:

" I bless the sun, I bless the moon,
And the stars that in heaven glitter;
And I also bless the little birds
That in the tree-tops twitter.

"I bless the sea, I bless the land,
And the dewy meads of clover;
I bless the violets,—mild as the eyes
Of my darling to her lover !—

"Those violet eyes of thine, my wife,
Now sending my soul to heaven !—
And I also bless the lilac-tree
Where thou to my arms wert given!"

SECRET AFFINITIES.

FROM THE FRENCH OF THÉOPHILE GAUTIER.

IN Athens, in a wall on high,
For centuries against the sky,
Twin marble blocks together gleamed,
Together slept, together dreamed.

The sea, whose tears for Venus fell,
Wrought of those tears, within a shell,
Two pearls that lay together prest,
And each to each their love confest.

In Boabdilla's gardens fair,
Where fountains cooled the summer air,

Two roses, blooming on one bough,
Made each to each a lover's vow.

In Venice, on an eve in May,
Two doves with white wings took their way
To one high nest within a dome,
Where love and they had built their home.

But pearl, dove, rose, and marble—all
Beneath one common fate did fall;
For pearl must melt, rose fade, dove die,
And marble crumble by and by.

But back to Nature's stock and store
Their dainty dust was flung once more,
And through her crucible was passed
And into fairer mouldings cast.

So wide her alchemy did range,
The marble into life did change;
The roses, that had died apace,
Did bloom again in woman's face;

The doves, that fluttered once, do still
True lovers' hearts with flutterings fill;
The pearls, once by the waves concealed,
Are now by maiden mouths revealed.

By this strange alchemy, whose worth
More precious is than all the earth,
Two souls, without the need of speech,
Are sure that each is knit to each.

A sudden beam of sunshine falls,
A sudden whiff of fragrance calls,
And by this sign true hearts, from far,
Like bees, meet where their gardens are.

Then all past whisperings in the ear,
Whether beside the fountain clear—
Beneath the wave—or in the wall,—
The heart that listens hears them all.

The doves, that part, shall not forget
The golden dome where first they met ;
For love, the first of Heaven's great laws,
All severed souls together draws.

And love, outgrown, a new life finds,
And to the past the present binds ;
And so, in lips of living red,
Awakes the rose that once was dead ;

And so the laugh of some fair girl
Unvails the long-sequestered pearl ;
And so her forehead in the light
Reveals the marble grown more white ;

And so the lover tells his love
Once more with cooings like the dove ;—
And so the whole of love's sweet lore
Repeats the tale of loves before.

Fair maid, before whose feet I fall,

What memories dear canst thou recall?

In some dim past did we not meet

As dove, or pearl, or rosebud sweet?

11

PYRRHA.

FROM THE LATIN OF HORACE.*

(A Paraphrase.)

WHAT youth, with roses round his brow,

And sweetly-scented drops bedewed,

Makes love to thee, O Pyrrha, now,

Within thy shady solitude?

What victim is it to ensnare

That thou dost bind thy yellow hair

In braids so simple yet so fair?

The fool, whoever he may be,

Who sets his silly heart on thee,

---

* Lib. I., Car. 5.

Shall find that never wooer wooed
A maid of such a fickle mood;
For thou art changeful as the skies:
At first, he sees them azure-hued,
But then, before he is aware,
The elements are all at feud,—
Wild mists and flying fogs arise,—
A tempest suddenly is brewed,
And thunder hurtles through the air!—
While he, fond wretch, stands shivering there,
With hopes storm-pelted and subdued,
And nothing left him but despair!

O luckless is the love-sick wight
Who trusts the troth which thou dost plight,
And whom thou flatterest to delude!
No sooner hath he knelt and sued,
And found thee gentle for a day,
Than he goes credulous away,
Till, with the next returning morn,

He hies him back to find thee rude,
And full of woman's wrath, and scorn,
And boisterous as when Capricorn
Roars through his stormiest latitude !

I too thy sunny smiles have viewed ;
I too have seen thy lightnings flash ;
I too have heard thy thunders crash ;
I too have felt thy wild waves dash ;
But I, (more blest by fate than he !)—
From out the depth of that deep sea
Came safe (yet dripping) from the main,—
To hang, in Neptune's sacred fane,
My votive offering on the wall,—
With thanks that I escaped at all !

THE KING OF THULÉ.

FROM THE GERMAN OF GOETHE.

I.

THERE was a king in Thulé,
  Who loved, with all his soul,
His leman who, in dying,
  Gave him a golden bowl.

II.

Beyond all other treasures
  This goblet did he prize,—
And when at feasts he filled it,
  The tears swam in his eyes.

III.

Then, feeling death approaching,
　His towns he counted up,
And gave his heir the kingdom—
　But not the golden cup!

IV.

He made a feast right royal,
　And with his knights sat he,—
In the high hall of his fathers,
　In the Castle by the Sea.

V.

There drank the old carouser
　His last draught, red as blood,
And then the hallowed flagon
　Flung down into the flood.

VI.

He watched it plunge, and settle,
And sink deep in the sea,—
And with it sank his eyelids,
And never more drank he !

FINALE.

Here, little book, thou comest to an end ;
Yet, ere thou sayst farewell, add one more rhyme ;
For since these Northern gales of autumn-time,—
That shrivel other leaves,—perchance portend
Like fate for thee (though this may Heaven forfend!)
Fly with these winds—which, in their antique prime,
First wafted Odin's runes from clime to clime—
And let thy flying leaves their rustlings blend,
For one brief moment, with that anthem vast
Whose rhythm eternal tunes the thunder's blast,
The linnet's warble, and the lover's sigh !
Nor grieve if then thy fleeting hour be past.
The bards are one, the lowly and the high !
That thou wert of them, be content and die !

APPENDIX.

11*

NOTES.

THOU AND I.

" Arcadia, whereof poets tell." p. 8.

THE original and real Arcadia (that is, the central region of the Peloponnesus) is far from justifying the ideal character with which the Roman poets and their successors have always invested it; for it neither was, nor is, a paradise of shepherds,—except in imagination. Instead of a region of lush meadows and blooming pasturage, Mitford calls it "a cluster of mountains;" Grote says, "it was high and bleak, full of wild mountain, rock, and forest;" and modern tourists familiarly style it "the Switzerland of Greece." But, however warlike or mercenary may have been the Arcadians of Strabo's day,—and however wild and desolate their country is now,—nevertheless the poetic fancy of the world will probably always cherish Arcadia as the spot where Hermes invented the lyre; where Pan gave to the shepherds their syrinx, or pipe ; and where a pastoral and musical people are forever chanting of love and peace.

" *Like sorrowing Clité.*"   p. 10.

Clité, a daughter of the sea, was in love with Apollo, god of the sun; but as the god's affections were bestowed elsewhere, the disappointed maiden yearned after him with hopeless grief ; and she is symbolized by the sunflower, whose face follows the sun across the sky.

" *Or jealous Amphitrité.*"   p. 10.

Amphitrité, wife of Neptune, grew jealous of her husband's love for Scylla, and, to revenge herself on her rival, threw a handful of magic herbs into the fountain wherein Scylla bathed,—which fretted the water, and transformed the beautiful and offending bather into a monster.

" *That wild herb of Trebizond.*"   p. 12.

Fabled of the Persian rhododendron.

> " *Nor grows that gloomy tree of woe,*
> *That fatal mistletoe.* etc.
>
> *   *   *   *   *
>
> *—as when Edda's bard*
> *Saw every pebble weep for Balder slain."* p. 13.

In the Scandinavian mythology, Balder (who is somewhat analogous to the Greek Apollo) was the god of sunshine and summer. His mother, to preserve his life against all possible enemies, exacted from all things in Nature, both animate and inanimate, an oath that he should receive no harm from any source whatever—whether from fire, water, beast, bird, stone, or bush. All these took the oath, except only the mistletoe—a plant which was accidentally overlooked. When nothing (as was supposed) could hurt Balder, it became a favorite amusement of the gods to hurl various of these oath-bound missiles at their smiling favorite, in order to see them fall harmlessly at his feet. In the midst of this pastime, Loki (or the Spirit of Evil) plucked up a mistletoe-tree, ánd carried it to Hoder, the god of winter,— who, being blind, had not joined in the sport. "Why do you not throw something at Balder?" asked Loki. "Because I am blind ; and, besides, I have nothing to throw," was Hoder's reply. Loki then craftily put the mistletoe into Hoder's hands, and guiding the blind god's uplifted arm, enabled him to take straight aim.   The fateful branch violently struck Balder, who fell dead at the blow.

After Balder's death, the Fates promised that if all created things would join in weeping for his loss, he then should be restored to life and the world.   All nature tenderly complied with this request,—men, beasts, birds, trees, and stones; all save one—an ogress named Thok, who was Loki in disguise.

This universal lamentation of Nature for the loss of Balder is beautifully chronicled in a common expression in daily use among the Icelanders, who, when the ground is beaded with dew, say, " The stones are weeping for Balder's death."

" *Nor font of bitter taste,—*
Like Marah."   p. 14.

Exodus 15 : 23.

" *Nor bog Serbonian.*"   p. 14.

Plutarch, in his Life of Antony, says :

" The Serbonian marsh (which the Egyptians call Typhon's breathing-hole) is, in all probability, water left behind by, or making its way through from, the Red Sea ; which is here [*i. e.*, near Pelusium] divided from the Mediterranean by a narrow isthmus."

Milton, in the second book of Paradise Lost, locates the famous marsh thus :

> "A gulf profound as that Serbonian bog
> Betwixt Damiatta and Mt. Casius old."

"*Nor vapor Acheronian.*"   p. 14.

Acheron, as a river of Hades, may be supposed to have engendered a vapor analogous to that which Lucretius assigns to Lake Avernus. Thus, *De Rerum Naturâ*, lib. 6, 820 :

"The regions of Avernus send up, from beneath, a vapor destructive to birds—a vapor in such abundance as to poison the body of the atmosphere."

"*Ere yet Apollo ceased to rove
Through Daphné's grove.*"   p. 14.

The celebrated grove of Daphné was at Daphné, near Antioch in Syria, and contained a magnificent temple to Apollo, erected in commemoration of his love for the nymph.

> " *Where Mimir, every morn,*
> *Once lifted high his dripping horn.*"   p. 14.

The Prose Edda of the Icelanders, in speaking of the tree Ygdrasil, and of Mimir's Well, says :

"Under the root that stretches out toward the Frost Giants, there is Mimir's Well, in which wisdom and wit lie hidden.   The guardian of this well is named Mimir.   He is full of wisdom, because he drinks the waters of the well from the horn Gyoll, every morning."

> " *To call the fairies from afar*
> *To Candahar.*"   p. 15.

The frequent mention of this geographical name, in recent military dispatches from Afghanistan, rudely disturbs the old association which Thevenot thus describes: "There is a part (says he) of Candahar called Peria, or *Fairyland.*"

> " *By Him who, when the world was young,*
> *Nine days upon Ygdrasil hung."* p. 16.

The world, with all its mysteries of life, death, and destiny,—in other words, the whole problem which the universe presents to the mind of man,—is boldly imaged by the Scandinavian poets in the form of a gigantic ash-tree called Ygdrasil; whose roots strike down into the lowest earth, and whose branches reach up into the loftiest heaven. On this majestic tree, the god Odin (who ranked next after the original Creator of all things) voluntarily hung for nine days, —having first pierced himself with a spear, in order that, with sensibilities thus keenly alive, and through sufferings thus painfully protracted, he might hear the secrets of nature and learn their subtle meanings. When he had thus mastered this mystical lore, he re-uttered it to mankind in rhythmic measures called *runes :* hence all the sounds of nature, whether of winds, waters, birds, or insects,—together also with man's minstrelsy of harp and voice,—all these various cadences are but repetitions or re-echoes of Odin's runes.

> " *As in Endymion's dale."* p. 17.

The story of the beautiful youth Endymion, who slept a

long sleep in a secluded glen on the side (or top) of Mt.
Latmos, where he was watched over by Selené, has received
many differing interpretations ; but probably Endymion was
the sun, as Selené was certainly the moon.

———

" Outgleaming all the pearls of Orm,
Outflashing all the gems of Ind."   p. 18.

The reader will recall the opening lines of the second book
of Paradise Lost :

" High on a throne of royal state, which far
Outshone the wealth of Ormus or of Ind."

———

" Hermon's dew-besprinkled hill."   p. 19.

Psalm 133 : 3.

———

" Gideon's fleece."   p. 20.

Judges 6 : 36 *et seq.*

" Castalia's näiad-haunted rill."   p. 19.

Col. Mure gives an account of a visit which he made to the site of ancient Delphi, and of the adjoining Castalian spring. We learn from him that the town is now called Castri ; and the spring, the fountain of St. John.   The bed of the torrent is in a fissure between two rocks.   The waters ooze at first in a scarcely perceptible streamlet from among loose stones, but soon swell into a considerable brook.

" Helicon's twin-watered mount."   p. 19.

The two fountains on Mt. Helicon were Aganippé and Hippocrené.   They still remain.   Leake, the explorer, has identified their site as on the east side of the mountain and near the present church and convent of St. Nicholas.   The fountains are about two miles apart.

" As round, and ripe, and splendid
As those Iduna watched and tended."   p. 27.

The Northman's goddess Iduna personated the spring-time.   During the long Norwegian winter, the gods (namely, the vital powers of nature) languished and declined ; and had it not been for the care with which Iduna (or the ever-recurring spring) revived and refreshed their wasted energy, they would have perished.

The pretty story that, on one occasion, Iduna and her apples were stolen and carried away, and that the gods were thereby left to grow wrinkled and hoary until she and her fruits could be found and brought back,—is told with great vivacity in the national poetry of the Icelanders. See the Prose or Younger Edda.

" *As if they grew by Eschol's brook.*"   p. 28.

The grapes of Eschol are, to this day, the wonder of the vineyards of Palestine.   Dr. H. B. Tristam, in the Natural History of the Bible, says :

" Clusters weighing ten or twelve pounds have been gathered.   The spies doubtless bore the clusters between them on a staff, that the splendid grapes might not be crushed.   With care and judicious thinning, it is well known that bunches weighing nearly twenty pounds can be produced.   Not only are the *bunches* remarkable for their weight, but the *individual grape* attains a size rarely reached elsewhere."

" On old Engeddi's terraced banks." p. 28.

Canticles 1 : 14.

Unlike the vineyards of Eschol, those of Engeddi are now extinct; but many of the terraces still remain.

———

" Of Judah's wine-press, flowing still. p. 28.

The ancient richness of Judea, in the production of wine, is attested in Genesis 49, 11 :

" Binding his foal unto the vine, and his ass's colt unto the choice vine; he washed his garments in wine, and his clothes in the blood of grapes."

And Dr. Tristam says :

" Though Judah no longer maintains this ancient pre-eminence, yet where the vine is cultivated in Southern Judea, it still surpasses, both in the size of its grapes, and the quality of its wine, the produce of other parts of the country."

———

" Or frosty windflower of the spring." p. 28.

The white anemoné.

" *Th' Iberian snow.*"   p. 28.

Ancient Iberia was the region which the Russians now call Georgia.

" *As Medina's maids relate.*"   p. 29.

It is an oriental legend that when Adam and Eve were expelled from Eden, they were allowed to carry with them but a single flower as a souvenir of the Happy Garden from which they were banished ; and this flower was the myrtle.

" *Or Jove's white wing
When he, a swan, in Leda's arms,*" etc.   p. 29.

Keats, in Endymion, speaks of

" Valley lilies, whiter still
Than Leda's love."

" *The holy Hebrew tale.*"   p. 29.

Genesis 40 *et seq.*

" Who holds the winds within His hand."   p. 32.

Proverbs 30 : 4.

" Their huge ship up the shore."   p. 42.

In Pindar's fourth Pythian ode, he says that the Argonauts carried their ship on their shoulders, for twelve successive days, over the desert sands of Libya.

" How writhingly were wrought
The. twelve great toils."   p. 42.

The myth of Hercules and his twelve labors is interpreted by the Rev. G. W. Cox as follows :

"Heracles is the *toiling sun*, laboring for the benefit of others, not his own, and doing hard service for a mean and cruel taskmaster.   *   *   *   His toils are variations on the story of the great conflict which Indra wages against Vitra, the demon of darkness."—*Tales of Ancient Greece.*

" Of him who in the viewless net."   p. 42.

The story of the invisible yet infrangible net which the

jealous Vulcan wrought, in order to ensnare in it the unsus-
pecting lovers, Mars and Venus,—is told in the eighth book
of the Odyssey.

" Of him who evermore uprolled
Th' enchanted stone that slipped his hold."   p. 42.

If every story in the Greek mythology is but a poetic
representation of some phenomenon of Nature (as modern
criticism is more and more vigorously asserting)—then the
repetitious labors of Sisyphus with his stone may be taken
as another of the many pictures of the daily rising and
setting of the sun,—to rise and set again.

" How Jove, in wrath, the Titans hurled
Down-whizzing to the lower world."   p. 43.

The Titanomachia, or contest of Jupiter with the Titans,
took place in Thessaly ;—the Titans occupying Mt. Orthrys,
and Jupiter, Mt. Olympus. The struggle lasted ten years ;
at the end of which time the Titans were hurled into Tar-
tarus.

" How Ossa was on Pelion flung."   p. 43.

In the war between the giants and the gods, the giants piled Mt. Ossa on Mt. Pelion, in the vain hope thereby to scale Mt. Olympus.   In Holland's Travels in Greece, he states that Ossa and Pelion, when seen from the south, look as if one mountain rested upon the other.   There is an ancient tradition that both mountains were originally one, and were rent apart by an earthquake.

———

" How Arthur's sword was three times swung."   p. 43.

In the Idyls of the King, after King Arthur's sword Excalibur was cast forth toward the lake,

> "—ere he dipped the surface, rose an arm
> Clothed in white samite, mystic, wonderful,
> And caught him by the hilt and brandished him
> Three times, and drew him under in the mere."

———

> *" Charlemagne's battle-brand,—*
> *Which he alone could hold,—*
> *Too ponderous for another's hand."*   p. 43.

The legend that Charlemagne bore a sword so huge and

12

heavy that no other warrior could wield it, is somewhat dwarfed of its heroic proportions by the moderate-sized weapon now exhibited in the Louvre, purporting to have belonged to that monarch.

" Samson at the gates."   p. 45.

Judges 16 : 3.

" For us, the almond-tree
Doth flourish now."   p. 49.

Ecclesiastes 12 : 5.

The almond-tree is an emblem of old age because (as Hasselquist has pointed out) "the white flowers blossom on the bare branches."

" Olive, oak, or bay."   p. 49.

A crown of olive was given to the victor in the Olympic games ; a crown of bay (that is, laurel) to the victor in the

Pythian ; and a crown of oak to him who saved the life of a
Roman citizen in battle.

––––––

" *Our threescore years and ten,*" etc.   p. 49.

                              Psalm 90 : 10.

––––––

" *For Mamré's gloomy cave,*
To be her grave."   p. 50.

                              Genesis 23.

––––––

"*Mt. Nebo.*"   p. 50.

                              Deuteronomy 34.

––––––

" *The King of Thulé's golden cup.*   p. 53.

See Margaret's song in Goethe's Faust, metrically translated at page 245 of this volume.

––––––

" *Ghizeh's time-defying graves.*"   p. 53.

After much controversy, it is now generally conceded that

the pyramids were built for royal tombs and monuments. Sharpe, in his History of Egypt, speaking of Memphis, says :

"Sixty or seventy pyramids, of various sizes, on the edge of the desert, remind us of the number and wealth of its kings or chief priests, who sleep beneath them."

And, referring to the custom of burying treasures within the mummies of the dead, he says :

"Gold and precious stones were often wrapped in the same bandages with the body."

" *Seen from Patmos by the seer.*"   p. 56.

The island of Patmos,—to which St. John was exiled by the Roman government, and where, according to a tradition of the Church, he wrote the Apocalypse,—is one of the Sporades, in the Greek Archipelago. Its modern name is Patmo. Travelers are pointed to a spot on the side of a hill, not far from a Greek monastery; as the place where the seer stood when he beheld the vision of the Holy City.

See Revelation 21 : 2.

> " *Each equaling each,*
> *Whichever way the reed could reach.*"   p. 57.

The figure of a cube seems to have been, to the oriental mind, a symbol of ideal beauty in architecture,—as is shown not only by St. John's description of the proportions of the Celestial City, but also by the plan both of the Jewish tabernacle, and of the Mahommedan Kaába.

> " *Himmaldya's crest.*"   p. 57.

Its height is nearly 29,000 feet.

> " *Hecla's burning pile*
> *Whose smoke rolls up for many a lofty mile.*"   p. 57.

This volcano has been known to throw up a column of ashes nearly four miles high.

> " *Tenerif's cloud-confronting isle.*"   p. 57.

The peak of Tenerif reaches to a height of 12,280 feet.

" *The Five Cities of the Plain.*"   p. 58.

These were Sodom, Gomorrah, Admah, Tseboim, and Zoar ; of which the first four were destroyed, and only the last escaped.

" *Their engulphing main.*"   p. 58.

The opinion so long held, that the Cities of the Plain were swallowed up by the Dead Sea, has been re-affirmed by some modern travelers, but disputed by others. Thus Robinson says that the cities were submerged ; but Reland insists that there is no reason, either in Scripture or history, for supposing that the cities were destroyed by submersion, or were submerged at all.

" *Th' asphaltic flood.*"   p. 58.

On the shores of the Dead Sea, bitumen or (asphaltum) is found in large quantities. Mr. Tristam, in his account of a visit there, says that bitumen is ejected from the bottom of the sea—floats in great masses on the surface of the water—oozes through the fissures of the rocks—and is deposited with gravel on the beach. It is sometimes called Jews' pitch.

> " *Upon whose banks there groweth,*
> *On either side,*
> *The Tree of Life, whose branches midway meet*
> *To overarch the amber tide.*" p. 59.

Revelation 22 : 2.

Dr. Adam Clarke, in his Commentary, says :

" As this Tree of Life is stated to be in the streets of the city, and on each side of the river, the *tree* must here be an enallage of the singular for the plural number, *trees of life*, or trees which yielded fruit by which life was preserved. The account in Ezekiel (chap. 47 : 12) is this: ' And by the river upon the bank thereof, on this side and on that side, shall grow all trees for meat, whose leaf shall not fade; it shall bring forth new fruit according to his months; and the fruit thereof shall be for meat, and the leaf thereof for medicine.' "

> " *That amaranthine flower.*" p. 59.

Milton's allusion to the amaranth is the following :

" Immortal amarant, a flower which once
In Paradise, fast by the Tree of Life,
Began to bloom ; but soon for man's offence
To Heaven removed, where first it grew, there grows,
And flowers aloft, shading the fount of life,
And where the river of bliss through midst of Heaven
Rolls o'er Elysian flowers her amber stream."

P. L., book 3, line 353 *et seq.*

Hume, in a note on the above passage from Milton, describes the amaranth as—

"A flower of a purple velvet color, which, though gathered, keeps its beauty ; and, when all other flowers fade, recovers its lustre by being sprinkled with a little water, as Pliny affirms. Milton seems to have taken this hint from 1 Peter 1 : 4, ' To an inheritance incorruptible, undefiled, and that *fadeth not away*,' (*amaranton:*) and chap. 5 : 4, ' Ye shall receive a crown of glory that *fadeth not away*,' (*amarantinon :*) both relating to the name of his everlasting amarant, which he has finely set near the tree of life. ' *Amarantus flos, symbolum est immortalitatis.'—Clem. Alex.*"

" *As in the parable is told.*"   p. 61.

St. Matthew 13 : 46.

" The gates shall not be shut by day,
And there is no night there." p. 61.

Revelation 21 : 25.

" The first, a jasper." p. 63.

The Rev. William Latham Bevan, M.A., in Smith's Dictionary of the Bible says :

" The characteristics of this stone, as far as they are specified in Scripture (Rev. 21 : 11) are that it was 'most precious,' and 'like crystal.' The stone which we name jasper does not accord with this description : it is an opaque species of quartz, of a red, yellow, green, or mixed brownish-yellow hue, sometimes striped and sometimes spotted, and in no respects presenting the characteristics of the crystal. There can be no doubt that the *diamond* would more accurately answer to the description in the book of Revelation. * * * We are disposed to think that the *diamond* is meant."

" Th' Tyrrhenian waves." p. 63.

The deep, bright blue of the Mediterranean Sea led Prof.

12*

Tyndall to make some interesting experiments as to the cause of the intense color.

" *That old City of the Blind.*"   p. 64.

Different reasons are given why ancient Chalcedon was called the City of the Blind: one is, that it was founded by a colony of blind men—a notion'which is sufficiently refuted by its own absurdity: another is, that the settlers, though not literally, were metaphorically blind, because they heedlessly chose a bad situation, when, if they had kept their eyes open, they could not have failed to see and choose the neighboring and more beautiful spot which was afterward occupied by Constantinople.

" *The fifth, a sard.*"   p. 64.

In King James's version, the word for the fifth stone is sardonyx. But as Josephus, in one place, says that the first stone in the High-Priest's Breastplate was the sardius, and, in another place, that it was the sardonyx, the implication is that sardius and sardonyx were two names for the same stone. The Rev. William Houghton, in the Dictionary of the Bible, writes :

" As sardonyx is merely another variety of agate, to which also sardius belongs, there is no great discrepancy in the statement of the Jewish historian."

C. W. King, M.A., in his Natural History of Gems, speaking of the sard, sardius, or oriental carnelian, says:

" Of the modern *carnelian* the derivations are numerous, the usual one being assigned from its color of raw flesh, *carneus*."

" *The sixth, a ruby.*" p. 64.

The common version reads, "The sixth, sardius;" but the original word, which is here rendered *sardius*, is elsewhere, in the same version, rendered *ruby*.

" *Like th' ensanguined wine
That filled the Holy Grail.*" p. 64.

Dunlop, in his History of Fiction, says:

"St. Grael, or Sangrael, so called from Grasal, which signifies a cup in old French, or from the *Sanguis Realis* [the blood of Christ] with which it was supposed to have been filled. * * * On the day of the Crucifixion, Joseph of Ari-

mathea obtained possession of the *Hanap*, or cup, from
which his Master had, on the preceding evening, drunk with
his Apostles.   Before he interred the body of our Saviour, he
filled the vessel with the blood which flowed from His
wounds ; but the exasperated Jews soon afterward deprived
him of this holy relic, and sent him to a prison in the neighborhood of Jerusalem.   Here his departed Master appeared
to him, and comforted his captivity by restoring the sacred
Hanap.   At length, in the forty-second year of his confine-
ment, he was freed from prison by Titus, the Roman Empe-
ror.   After his deliverance, he proceeded to preach the
Gospel in this country [Great Britain].   After the arrival of
Joseph with the sacred cup in Britain, the romance is chiefly
occupied with the miracles accomplished by the Sangrael ;
the preparation of the Round Table of Arthur, who left a
vacant place for this relic ; and, finally, the achievements
performed by his knights to recover this treasure, which had
fallen into the hands of king Pecheur, so called from his
celebrity as an angler, or his notoriety as a sinner."

" *The eighth, a beryl.*"   p. 64.

Mr. Houghton writes :

" It is impossible to say, with any degree of certainty, what precious stone is denoted by the Hebrew word (*Tarshish.*) Luther reads the turquoise ; the Septuagint supposes either the chrysolite, or the carbuncle ; Onkelos and the Jerusalem have *kerum jama*, by which the Jews appear to have understood a ' *white stone*, like the froth of the sea.' "

" *Like Lilith, Adam's earlier bride*
Ere Eve was moulded from his side."   p. 65.

The Kabála has a myth that Adam, in Paradise, had a wife named Lilith, who dwelt with him before the creation of Eve.   This "earlier bride" is rarely mentioned by poets, but Rosetti has the following lines :

" Of Adam's first wife Lilith, it is told
 (The witch he loved before the gift of Eve)
That, ere the snake's, her sweet tongue could deceive."

" *The eleventh, a jacinth.*"   p. 65.

The words jacinth and hyacinth are etymologically the same.

—Touching the differences of opinion among commentators on the twelve stones, Dr. Thomson, author of the Land and the Book, has these remarks :

" I venture to say that this donkey-boy coming to meet us could confound nine-tenths of Bible readers in America by his familiar acquaintance with the names, appearances, and relative value of the precious stones mentioned in the Word of God. St. John was not a scholar, nor a lapidary, and yet he is perfectly at home among precious stones, and without effort gives a list which has puzzled, and does still puzzle, our wisest scholars to understand. In our translation, and in every other with which I am acquainted, the same Hebrew word is made to stand for entirely different gems ; and lexicographers, commentators, and critics are equally uncertain."

———

" *To royal Shiraz leads.*"   p. 66.

Moore, in Lalla Rookh, speaks of

—" that courteous tree
Which bows to all who seek its canopy."

This tree, according to Niebuhr, is of the genus mimosa,

and "droops its branches whenever any person approaches it, seeming as if it saluted those who retire under its shade."

" *Where the rose-gardens are.*"   p. 66.

The rose-gardens of Shiraz were so famous among the Persians that the works of Saadi, the Persian poet (who lived in that city) were called " The Gulistan," or the rose-garden.

" *The pitcher at the fountain's rim.*"   p. 69.

Ecclesiastes 12 : 6.

THE CHANT CELESTIAL.

" *Till marble Memnon heard it and made answer.*"   p. 82.

The poetic story that the statue of Memnon, when smitten by the morning light, gave forth music, has a basis of truth in the fact that the stone,—which cools by night, to be heated again by day,—emits, during this daily process of contraction and expansion, certain crackling sounds ; and many

trustworthy travelers testify that they have heard these murmurs quite distinctly.

———

" *Upon the waters of Castalia's fount.*"　p. 87.
See note p. 19.

———

" *Till Odin heard them on the tree Ygdrasil.*"　p. 87.
See note p. 16.

———

THE GRAVE ON THE PRAIRIE.

" *And twinkled in reflection.*"　p. 100.

When a flower-clad prairie is perfectly level (as many are)
the sunshine is reflected from the flowers to the spectator
from as many points as from the multitudinous ripples of a
lake ; the general picture being far more bespangled than if
the same number of flowers were distributed over a rolling
country, or hill and vale.

" Because a live-oak grew hard by.

*   *   *   *   *

And long, gray moss, with mournful grace."   p. 101.

Gigantic live-oak trees, hung with trailing gray moss, are among the conspicuous objects which strike the eye of a traveler in the southern portion of the United States.

" Then, while the bison joined his herd."   p. 102.

The animal popularly called the buffalo belongs to zoology under the name of the bison.

" The startled rabbit bounded."   p. 102.

There is a species of rabbit peculiar to Texas.   It is called the Texan hare, or (vulgarly) " jackass rabbit ; " bearing the latter name because its ears (which are five or six inches long) are shaped like those of a donkey. These great rabbits are often larger than the dogs that hunt them.

" The cactus," etc.   p. 102.

Millions of these grotesque plants are scattered over the

prairies of Texas. Sometimes a cluster is so huge as to measure a hundred feet in circumference,—reaching to the height of a man's head on horseback, and even higher. The bristling spines protect the leaves against all enemies save mildews and worms.

" *No wanderer ever went that way*
Except some cattle-ranger."   p. 103.

It is no uncommon thing in Texas for a man to own ten, fifteen, or twenty thousand head of cattle and as many horses ; putting to shame the meagre flocks and herds of the patriarchs of the Old Testament. The Texan herdsmen, who look after these immense droves, range on horseback over hundreds of miles of wild prairie.

" *Whose year is un-Decembered.*"   p. 105.

Although this expression is somewhat exaggerated, still in the neighborhood of San Antonio, and in many other localities in Texas, settlers who live in small, thatched cabins are frequently seen at night sleeping out of doors in mid-winter.

PRINCE AND PEASANT.

" *The King of Bernicia,*" etc.   p. 127.

Bernicia was the old name for that part of Britain which contained what are now called the Cheviot Hills and the River Tweed.

THE KING'S COURAGE.

" *The king—who loved two women—both at once.*"   p. 225.

The historic incident on which this *jeu d'esprit* is founded is given by Plutarch in his Life of Dion.

TRANSLATIONS.

SIR OLAF.

p. 231.

THIS translation from Heine reproduces the various metres of the original, and endeavors to be as close and literal as the difference in the two languages will permit.

PYRRHA.

p. 242.

The critical reader, who may be jealous of any tampering with Horace, is reminded that this is not offered as a translation, but as a paraphrase.

THE KING OF THULÉ.

P. 245.

The beautiful original of Goethe's " King of Thulé" is but faintly reflected in any of its numerous English renderings ; certainly in none of those which vainly aim at literalness ; and the present translator, in his rather free handling, does not flatter himself that he has done better than his predecessors in this difficult kind of work.

FINIS.